Teenagers *and* Compulsive Gambling

Teenagers and Compulsive Gambling

By Edward F. Dolan

FRANKLIN WATTS
New York   Chicago   London   Toronto   Sydney

The author wishes to acknowledge permission to quote from the following sources:

Robert Custer and Harry Milt, *When Luck Runs Out: Help for Compulsive Gamblers and Their Families*, New York: Facts on File Publications, 1985.
Henry R. Lesieur, *The Chase: Career of the Compulsive Gambler*, Rochester, Vermont: Schenkman Books, 1984.
Henry R. Lesieur, *Understanding Compulsive Gambling*, Center City, Minn.: Hazelden Foundation, 1986.

Library of Congress Cataloging-in-Publication Data

Dolan, Edward F., 1924–
     Teenagers and compulsive gambling / by Edward F. Dolan.
        p.   cm.
     Includes bibliographical references and index.
     ISBN 0-531-11100-8
     1. Compulsive gambling—United States—Juvenile literature.
     2. Teenagers—United States—Juvenile literature.   [1. Gambling.]
     I. Title.
     HV6715.D63   1994
     362.2'5—dc20   93-31956 CIP AC

CONTENTS

Teenagers *and* Compulsive Gambling

ACKNOWLEDGMENTS

I am deeply indebted to many fine people for their assistance in the preparation of this book. For providing me with needed research materials and/or patiently answering my questions, my appreciation must go to Dr. Henry R. Lesieur, professor of sociology, Saint John's University, Jamaica, New York; Dr. Valerie C. Lorenz, executive director, National Center for Pathological Gambling, Baltimore; Jean Falzon, executive director, the National Council on Problem Gambling, New York City; Karen H., international executive director, Gamblers Anonymous, Los Angeles; the Gam-Anon International Service Office, Whitestone, New York; and the Compulsive Gambling Rehabilitation Program, Charter Hospital, Las Vegas.

In addition, I must thank Dr. Lesieur for reviewing my manuscript and making many fine editorial comments and suggestions.

TEENAGE GAMBLING

Jan was bored with her life as a housewife. To break the monotony, she began betting on the horses at a racetrack near her California home and was delighted when she won several hundred dollars in just a few weeks. She then got in touch with a bookmaker who took wagers on horse races throughout the country. But now she began to lose—steadily. And now she found herself spending more and more as she tried to recover her losses. Soon all she could think of was gambling. Her husband flew into a rage when she took $7,000 from a savings account that was meant for their daughter's college education and lost it. He told Jan to stop gambling or he would leave her.

In 1990 the police in Pennsauken, New Jersey, arrested Ben on suspicion of burglary. During later questioning, Ben admitted to stealing $10,000 in items from his home and others in the city. He said that he had been forced to steal to make good his gambling debts.[1]

These are true stories, though the names given to the two gamblers are fictitious. Both Jan and Ben have damaged their lives with their continual and excessive betting. Both are known as compulsive gamblers, meaning that they are addicted to gambling and that the placing of their "next bet" is even more important to them than eating. They will go to any lengths to raise the money for it.

As gamblers, the two differ in only one way: Jan is an adult; Ben is a teenager. He is part of a phenomenon that is being seen as a new American problem—the spread of gambling among the nation's young people. Some experts observing the personal disasters caused by gambling predict that it is destined to become the major youth problem of the 1990s, forging ahead of such current tragedies as drug and alcohol abuse and teenage pregnancy. Among those making the prediction are psychiatrists, psychologists, doctors, social workers, and ex–compulsive gamblers.[2]

♥ WHY THE GROWING NUMBER OF TEEN GAMBLERS?

Why is there a growing number of teen gamblers in the United States? As the experts in gambling problems see things, the answer is simple: More and more American adults have been turning to gambling in recent years. As can be expected, a growing number of teenagers are following their example.

But why have more and more Americans been turning to gambling?[3] Again, in the eyes of the experts, the answer is simple: Gambling is currently being made legal in more and more states. Consequently, many people who would have nothing to do with an illegal activity now feel free to try their hand at betting.

Gambling laws in the United States are not set by the federal government but are left to the states. There was a time not too long ago when most gambling activities were illegal in the country, with the chief exceptions being horse and dog racing in a number of states and casino gambling in Nevada and the U.S.-held island of Puerto Rico. Gambling was banned as illegal in response to a variety of views held by countless Americans. For one, it was seen as a waste of time and money; people had to be protected from an enterprise that almost always separated them from their hard-earned money. Second, it was condemned as immoral; it fostered the desire to get something without working for it, an attitude that ran contrary to the age-old tradition that the worthwhile things in life are to be gained through hard and honest toil.

In brief, great segments of the American public held that gambling was not respectable and that those who participated in it were themselves not quite respectable—and sadly foolish to boot. This view was not confined to the United States. It was, as we'll see in later chapters, shared by many people in other parts of the world.

But recent years have brought a change of attitude in the United States. Widely blamed for the change are the lotteries that an increasing number of states are now sponsoring. A lottery comes in many forms, but is basically a game in which the players purchase tickets printed with sets of numbers. The sponsors of the lottery then draw numbers at random from a barrel or some other storage device. The winners are those whose tickets have some combination of numbers that match the ones drawn. The players are awarded cash prizes on the basis of how many of the matching numbers appear on their tickets. The prizes can range from a low of five dollars for, say, three matching numbers to millions of dollars for tickets containing all the matching numbers.

Some twenty-five years ago only one state—New Hampshire—conducted a lottery. New Hampshire was joined five years later by the state of New York. Today thirty-three states, the District of Columbia, Puerto Rico, and the American-held Virgin Islands all conduct lotteries. They do so as a means of raising funds needed for public education, highway construction, and other projects without raising taxes. The funds are raised by setting aside for government use a portion of the money that comes in from the sale of lottery tickets.

Supporters of the lotteries call them "fun" and a "painless" kind of taxation. Lottery critics condemn them as a waste of money, a "losers' game," saying that the odds against winning a top prize are astronomical. In a lottery in which a player attempts to pick six out of fifty-four numbers, for example, the odds against choosing the correct six are 12.9 million to 1.

The critics further argue that the lotteries are making gambling respectable and that the fantastic top prizes are enticing an ever-mounting number of Americans to try to get something for nothing, without working for it. They also argue that the huge amounts brought in by the lotteries have caused a number of states to legalize other forms of gambling as a further means of raising money.

At present, including those that sponsor lotteries, forty-eight of our fifty states permit some form of gambling, gambling that ranges from horse and dog racing to bingo, card playing, and betting on sports competitions. New Jersey in 1979 joined Nevada in allowing casino gambling. Several of the states that border the Mississippi River have authorized casino gambling aboard the tourist boats that ply the river, a throwback to the nineteenth century, when, as we'll see later, professional gamblers were daily seen aboard all the river's paddle wheelers. The only states that have no legalized gambling are Utah and Hawaii.

The critics contend that, as a consequence of all this, adult and teenage Americans everywhere are being encouraged to try their hand at every type of gambling and that a growing number are responding to the encouragement in the hope of making a quick and easy win. The situation has become so bad, the critics claim, that the nation is now caught in the grip of a "gambling fever."

On at least two counts they seem to be right. First, the Center for Addiction Studies at Harvard University told *Time* magazine in 1989 that the proportion of American adults who gamble occasionally stood at 60 percent in 1969. It had jumped to 81 percent by the end of the next twenty years, according to a national poll taken by the Gallup organization. *Time* reported that some experts believe the proportion to be as high as 88 percent.

Second, the money raked in by legal U.S. gambling has been mounting through recent years, rising to around $250 billion annually by the early 1990s. As huge as it is, however, that amount does not tell the full story. Millions more are known to be spent on illegal gambling—on back-alley dice and card games and at the tables in clandestine gambling halls in many of the states where casinos are not allowed.

There has always been illegal gambling in the United States because many people have chosen to ignore or defy the law. Gambling foes suspect that such play is now growing along with legal play and is, in fact, being pushed along by it. The belief is that countless Americans, caught up in the current gambling fever, are turning to illegal games in those areas where certain types of play are still banned.

Since illegal gambling is conducted in secret, the total amount of money wagered on it is unknown, but is estimated to run between $30 billion and $42 billion a year.

Later on, we'll talk more about the money being made by both legal and illegal gambling. But for now just let us say that, when the annual "take" is combined with the increasing number of players cited in the poll by the Gallup organization, there can be no doubt that growing numbers of Americans, young and old alike, are showing a willingness to risk their money on a bet.

♠ HOW WIDESPREAD IS TEEN GAMBLING?

No one knows exactly how many U.S. teenagers have taken up gambling. But we can get an idea of their number from several recent studies.[4] One is the work of Dr. Durand F. Jacobs of California. Dr. Jacobs is a clinical psychologist and professor at Loma Linda University Medical School. He is also a member of the board of directors of the National Council on Problem Gambling, an organization dedicated to helping troubled gamblers overcome their problems. His study was conducted over a four-year span at fifteen high schools in California, Connecticut, Minnesota, New Jersey, and Virginia.

The study involved 3,700 students. Dr. Jacobs learned that 50 percent of their number had gambled for money during a year's period. Eighty-two percent admitted that they had gambled by age fifteen. Thirty-two percent told him they had gambled as early as age eleven. As a result, he estimated that more than half of all young people age fourteen to seventeen have gambled at one time or another during the span of a year.

The doctor believes that the state lotteries are

much to blame for the increase in gambling among young people. He found that the number of California teenagers who gamble doubled between 1985 and 1987, the first two years in which the state's Lotto game was held.

Evidence of the extent of teen gambling also comes from Dr. Henry R. Lesieur and Robert Klein. In 1987 the two researchers developed a series of gambling questions and asked that they be answered by 892 eleventh- and twelfth-graders in four New Jersey high schools. Dr. Lesieur is a professor of sociology at Saint John's University in Jamaica, New York; Mr. Klein is an employee assistance program manager with Burke/Taylor Associates in Research Triangle Park, North Carolina, and was the executive director of the Council on Compulsive Gambling of New Jersey at the time of the survey. They reported the results of their survey in a 1987 issue of *Addictive Behaviors* magazine. They wrote that:

♦ 91 percent of the young people said they had gambled at least once in their lifetime.

♣ 86 percent admitted to gambling during the past year.

♥ 49 percent said they had played cards for money in the past year, with 6 percent playing once a week or more.

♠ 45 percent reported that they had wagered on state lotteries, and 13 percent had done so weekly.

♦ 32 percent acknowledged participating in some form of gambling at least once a week during the past year.

The United States is not alone in experiencing the spread of gambling among young people. In 1988 and 1989 the *Journal of Gambling Behavior*, a magazine sponsored by the National Council on Problem Gambling, reported the findings of research conducted in other countries:

In 1988, the Lesieur-Klein questions were asked of 1,612 students in nine high schools in the Canadian city of Quebec. The young people were ages fourteen to nineteen. Seventy-six percent said that they had gambled at least once in their life, with 65 percent acknowledging that they had placed a bet within the past year. Fifty-one percent reported betting less than once in a week, while 24 percent admitted placing a wager at least once a week.

A 1981 study of 136 boys in India showed that 68 percent of their number gambled and that 39 percent were regular gamblers; the boys ranged in age from seven to sixteen.

A survey of fifty British thirteen- and fourteen-year-olds in 1988 revealed that 89 percent of their number gambled. Both boys and girls were surveyed, with 93 percent of the boys and 84 percent of the girls admitting to gambling.

One aspect of the Lesieur-Klein study in New Jersey proved especially disturbing to many people—the fact that 46 percent of the students had managed to enter the state's casinos and that 3 percent had succeeded in playing there on a weekly basis.[5] The young people had gone undetected or had shown fake I.D. cards when challenged by casino employees.

Customers must be twenty-one years old before they are legally able to enter the casinos in Nevada and New Jersey. (In most states, an individual must be eighteen to participate in certain other forms of gambling, such as lotteries.) The casinos are often criticized for permitting underage players to enter, but argue that it is extremely difficult to spot some minors because they look twenty-one or older or have I.D. cards to show that they are of age. The casinos admit that a number of minors must assuredly get past the surveillance of a club's employees and security system, but they quickly point out that they sight and refuse admittance to or eject thousands of underage players each year.

The number of underage players turned away at the door or ejected from the casino floors tells us much about youth's growing interest in gambling. In Atlantic City the casinos claim that they presently refuse entrance to or eject some 29,000 underage players each month, for a total of around 348,000 a year. This total is substantially higher than those recorded in earlier years. In 1989, according to the National Council on Problem Gambling, the clubs denied entrance to about 230,000 underage players and ejected another 25,000, while the totals for 1987 were 197,842 denied entrance and 34,018 ejected.

♣ ANOTHER VIEW OF GAMBLING: A PLEASANT PASTIME

Though many Americans condemn gambling as a moral wrong or a waste of time and money, millions of others look on it as a pleasant and exciting pastime. They engage in informal and low-stakes card games, such as poker and gin rummy, at home. They participate in the various forms of gambling that are permitted by local and state laws. They may spend a weekend now and again at the Nevada and New Jersey casinos or drop by for a visit when passing through on vacation. They play bingo, perhaps weekly, at a church or some other community facility. They visit local racetracks to wager on horse and dog racing. Those who live in states that sponsor lotteries buy one or a number of tickets each week, hoping to win anywhere from a few dollars to millions. The tickets usually cost a dollar each.

Along with viewing gambling as a pleasant pastime, most of these Americans, who are known as social gamblers, share two major characteristics: They usually wager no more than they can afford, and they are able to stop betting when they decide they've lost enough.

To them, there is nothing wrong with gambling. They feel that, in itself, it is harmless. It can be compared to the automobile, which, in itself, is also quite harmless. The car does not become dangerous until a drunken or careless or foolhardy driver takes the wheel.

But there are gamblers who are no different from the driver who turns the automobile into a dangerous weapon. They are known as problem gamblers. They suffer from their problem to various degrees.

♥ PROBLEM GAMBLERS

Problem gambling can be compared to a scale. At one end of the scale are some problem gamblers who make foolish bets at times in an effort to reap a big win or get back money that they previously lost. Toward the middle of the scale are those who wager more at times than they can afford, on occasion *much* more, and put their families in a temporary or long-lasting financial bind.

The key phrase here is *at times*. It indicates that their gambling, while foolish and costly, is not a daily, uncontrollable habit.

At the most dangerous and tragic end of the scale are the gamblers whose habit *is* a daily matter and who are unable to control or end it. They do not limit themselves to sums they can afford to lose. They cannot stop gambling when they know they've had enough or are in danger of losing their very last dollar. To raise the money needed to feed their habit, some have stolen from their loved ones, broken into their family savings, burgled homes in their neighborhoods and elsewhere, engaged in shady schemes and business deals to cheat friends and strangers alike, robbed at gunpoint, and embezzled funds from their companies.

Like Jan and Ben, whose stories were told at the start of this chapter, these are the compulsive gamblers, or as they are often called in psychiatry and psychology, the pathological gamblers. They are as addicted to gambling as the alcoholic is to liquor, the "hooked" smoker to cigarettes, and the drug addict to heroin or cocaine. They feel powerless in the grip of their habit and seem helpless to keep from making their next bet.

There are no statistics to show the exact number of compulsive gamblers in the nation, partly because so many compulsives do not step forward and admit their problem. We do, however, have some estimates.[6] Both the National Council on Problem Gambling and Gamblers Anonymous (a worldwide self-help organization for compulsives seeking to be rid of their problem) believe the figure to be approximately 10 million. A slightly smaller figure is given by *Time* in a 1991 article on gambling; the magazine reported researchers as saying that some 8 million Americans are compulsive players. *Time* added that, of those 8 million people, at least 1 million are teenagers.

If the estimates of 8 to 10 million are on the mark, then the spread of legal gambling in recent years has brought a significant increase in the number of compulsive players. In 1976 the Commission on the Review of the National Policy toward Gambling reported that there were an estimated 1.1 million compulsive gamblers in the country at that time. Both Gamblers Anonymous and the National Council on Problem Gambling disputed this approximation as too low. They said that the 1976 figure was more likely 6 million. (The Commission was formed by Congress in the early 1970s to recommend official positions for the federal government in regard to gambling.)

♠ TEEN PROBLEM GAMBLING

Problem gambling with its many degrees of trouble looms as a special danger for teenagers because of the enthusiasm and daring that go hand in hand with being young. Most teenagers are far less cautious than the average adult. Even if young people never become compulsive gamblers, their enthusiasm and daring can lead to foolish betting and to spending more and more in the hope of recouping earlier losses or of feeling the heady elation that comes with winning. Dr. Durand Jacobs, on the basis of his four-year study, estimates that teenagers are two and a half times more likely than adults to become problem gamblers.[7]

Problem gambling among teenagers is new on the American scene. It was virtually unknown a decade ago. But now, according to the *Time* report in 1991, gambling counselors say that 7 percent of their cases concern young people with a gambling habit that is causing them trouble.[8]

Further word of problem gambling among the young comes from Minnesota. There, a study has found that more than 6 percent of all the state's youths between fifteen and eighteen suffer from problem gambling.[9]

Suffering most are the nation's young people who have become compulsive gamblers. They are caught in a habit that is painfully hard to break and also involves destructive behavior. Ben's theft of $10,000 to finance his habit serves as a case in point.

But Ben's story is far from being the most tragic case on record. His story is matched by that of a Philadelphia man who began gambling as a teenager and soon found himself placing horse-racing and other sports bets with bookmakers to the tune of $200 a week. In time his losses mounted to $5,000 and the bookmakers began to press for payment. He remembers that one threatened to "cut off my mother's legs" if he didn't come up with what he owed. Despite such threats, he went on gambling. Recently he lost his job when he was discovered embezzling funds from his company to support his betting.[10]

A 1989 case involved members of a championship high school football team in Texas. They and their friends were apprehended and sentenced for a series of armed robberies. In part, they had committed the crimes to pay off losses incurred in campus dice games.

One publicized case concerns an Atlantic City teenage girl who played steadily at the city's casinos in the 1980s.[11] Over several years, she gambled away more than $5,000, some of it her money, some of it her family's. Among her losses were funds that had been set aside for her college education. Because she was a heavy bettor—a "high roller"—the casinos gave her various favors, including free hotel rooms, meals, and limousine rides.

In 1987 her father, an Atlantic City detective, complained to authorities and demanded that his daughter be barred from the casinos. To help the clubs identify her, he provided them with photographs of the girl. He also urged the state to bring charges of allowing underage gambling against five casinos.

For a time the clubs, accidentally or carelessly, failed to turn the teenager away, even though armed with the identifying photos. But her father's efforts finally proved successful and the girl was barred from play. Faced with the charge of permitting underage gambling, the five casinos contributed $180,000 to mental health clinics for the treatment of compulsive gambling.

But, in her father's opinion, these actions came too late. He claimed that by the time his daughter was barred from the clubs, she had become addicted to gambling.

♦ A FINAL POINT

Much of this book will concentrate on those most tragic of young figures—the compulsive gamblers—and will talk of how their gambling habit develops and usually extends into their adulthood, of how it harms not only them but also their families and friends, of what they can do to break free, and of where they can turn for help when they finally decide that they must somehow start life afresh.

But it is also the aim of this book to do something else—namely, to help the families and friends who are suffering because of the actions of the compulsive gambler in their midst.

To see how the book will seek to achieve this aim, let us suppose for a moment that you are not a compulsive gambler but rather the child of a compulsive gambler. As you read the chapters on how the gambling habit takes root, grows, and contorts the personality of the player, you'll come to a better understanding of what is happening to your parent, and you'll see why he or she is behaving in certain ways. And when you reach the chapters on how the teenage compulsive's parents and the adult's spouse and children (remember, the teen compulsion usually extends into adulthood) are made to suffer, you'll see more clearly what the people in your own home—your non-gambling parent, your brothers and sisters, and you yourself—are going through. Perhaps most important of all, you'll come to know that you as the child of a compulsive gambler are not suffering alone. Your feelings are not unique; they are shared by millions of young people not only across our country but throughout the world.

Knowing all this may help you live successfully through your problems with your compulsive parent. Finally, the concluding chapters on how the compulsive can work to start life afresh, and where he or she can seek help, will contain information that should be of assistance in putting your problems behind you.

Now, before we can give our full attention to teenage compulsive gamblers, we need to see how gambling has held the people of all nations in its sway throughout the history of the world. We will then better understand the forces that are tempting more and more young Americans to gamble and run the risk of leading troubled lives.

GAMBLING THROUGH THE AGES

No one knows when gambling began. The world's earliest people left behind no records of when the first bets were placed. It is widely believed, however, that gambling dates back to the dawn of time and that the spectators at tribal sporting events may have started things off by wagering on the outcome of footraces. Over the centuries, the ancients developed games such as chess, dice, and cards in which contestants could gamble against one another. Any of these games could also be played just for fun, and very often were.

Though we are without written accounts of the world's earliest days, we have other indications of how old gambling may be. Archaeologists in Africa, Asia, Europe, and the Americas have unearthed age-old objects that seem to be the forerunners of today's dice—colored stones, animal bones, shells, and pieces of wood and ivory with figures and markings carved into their sides. Some, like today's dice, are cube-shaped; others have four flat sides and rounded ends; still others, such as wafer-thin strips of wood used by the North American Indians more than a thousand years ago, have just two faces.

♣ GAMBLING AFTER THE WRITTEN WORD

The origins of gambling are lost in the mists of time, but when human beings learned to record the story of their lives through writing and the drawing of pictures, they left us in no doubt that gambling was a familiar activity in virtually all cultures. To see how familiar, we need only look at three early civilizations.[1]

♥ Egypt

Paintings, artifacts, and the written word all attest to the fact that the early Egyptians gambled. Left for us to see, for example, is an ancient mural of two Egyptians playing a guessing game called atep. The players stand with their backs to each other, with a referee stationed between them. One player extends a number of fingers. The opponent then must try to guess their number. The referee keeps score of the correct and incorrect guesses and, of course, makes sure that the players do not cheat.

A similar game is still found throughout the world. Matches now usually serve in place of fingers.

But what of artifacts? At a museum in Berlin, Germany, are dice that Egyptians held in their hands 3,500 years ago. And, as old as these dice are, they are far from the oldest yet found. That distinction may belong to dice-like objects that have been found in Mesopotamia, the land of several ancient cultures. The Mesopotamian dice are shaped like pyramids and are at least five thousand years old.

On coming to the written word, we find one of

the most interesting legends in the history of gambling. It tells of how a wager gave the Egyptians a year of 365 days. The story is etched in hieroglyphics on a clay tablet discovered in the Great Pyramid of Cheops. The massive Pyramid stands at Giza near the city of Cairo and was constructed sometime around 3000 B.C. Here is the story told on the tablet:

Ra was the god of the sun and thus one of the greatest of all the Egyptian deities. He became furious one day when he learned that Nut, goddess of the sky, had fallen in love with and married her twin brother, Geb, the god of the earth. Ra ordered that the two be separated and that Nut should never bear a child on any day of the year. At the time, the Egyptians divided the year into 360 days.

Word of Nut's punishment reached Thoth, the god of the night. Thoth was a kindly god, and the news filled him with pity for the goddess Nut. And so he undertook a gamble on her behalf. He challenged the moon to roll dice with him, with the stakes for each game to be a fraction of moon's light. After Thoth had won a number of games, he divided his winnings into five new days, added them to the 360-day year, and gave them to Nut. Since they were new, they were outside Ra's authority, and Nut was able to use them to produce children. In time, she gave birth to five children, the gods Isis, Osiris, Horus, Nepthys, and Set.

♠ GREECE

A statue shows us that the ancient Greeks played a dice game. The statue depicts two women kneeling and preparing to flick an astragal to the ground between them. An astragal was an oblong object about the size of two modern dice cubes glued together. Made from the anklebone of a cloven-footed animal, usually a sheep, it had either two or four flat sides and rounded ends. Etched into its flat sides were mysterious figures and markings.

The astragal is thought to have been first used in Greece for divination, the foretelling of the future. The Greeks believed that everything in the world was controlled by the gods, and so the players tossed the astragal to see what the deities planned for them. The figures and markings that landed faceup delivered the message—perhaps one of good or bad luck, perhaps one of health or sickness. When a two-faced astragal was tossed, it gave the player a yes or no answer to a question about the future. Four-sided astragals provided more detailed messages.

In time this method of fortune-telling became a gambling game. The winner of each throw of the astragal was the player who received the best message for the future.

The Greeks were not alone in using dice-like objects for both gambling and divination. The reading of the future through the tossing of stones or bits of bone was practiced in many ancient societies. The Korean people shot arrows marked with various symbols into the air and either bet on how the arrows would land or looked for signs of what lay ahead in the way they actually did land.

The Greeks also had a game called black-and-white. The name derived from the fact that it was played with a flat stone or shell colored black on one side and white on the other. The participants flipped it into the air and bet on which side would land faceup.

The Greeks also created a gambling legend of their own. It tells of how the three mightiest Greek gods divided the universe among themselves by throwing dice. The god Zeus won the heavens. Poseidon won the sea, while Hades claimed the underworld.

♦ Rome

The Romans were among the most avid of the ancient world's gamblers. They played at dice. They wagered on chariot races, bullfights, and boxing and wrestling matches. And they developed the idea of using lotteries as a means of raising public funds.

Their thirst for gambling can be seen in their wagering on chariot races. The Roman historian Tacitus (A.D. 55–120) wrote that wealthy gamblers often bet so heavily on the chariots that some lost their entire fortune—homes, money, everything—on a single race.

Lotteries were favored by many Roman emperors, who used them for a variety of purposes. Emperor Augustus Caesar (63 B.C.–A.D. 14) sponsored Rome's first public lottery as a means of raising money to have the city's streets and public buildings repaired. Other emperors included lotteries as part of public festivals. Emperor Nero (A.D. 37–68) turned to a form of the lottery—the raffle—as a way to enliven parties by awarding gifts to his honored guests. The prizes could be slaves, horses and chariots, and even homes.

Romans, whether rich or poor, learned to gamble at an early age. They often started with ship-and-head, a game that was identical to the Greek black-and-white. The game was named ship-and-head because it was played with a coin that had a ship's prow etched on one side and the head of the god Janus on the other. (January is named for him.)

Another Roman game of chance can be seen in the story of the Roman soldiers who threw dice for the robe of Jesus Christ as he hung dying on the cross. Some historians think that the soldiers may have gambled for the robe with a game called ten. If so, they threw three dice with dots on their faces.

The winner was the player whose dice showed ten or more dots on landing.

♣ CENTURIES OF GAMBLING

Though we have described the play in three ancient cultures, historical records show that gambling was known in virtually all of the world's early societies.[2] Here, to prove the point, are stories from a series of widely separated regions:

In A.D. 1000, when Norse explorer Leif Ericson visited what is now Nova Scotia, he found the Indians there playing a stick game. The participants stood in a circle around the stick, which was then spun on an axis. The player at which the stick was pointing when it came to rest was declared the winner and scooped up all the objects or money that had been wagered on the spin.

The South American Indians were among the many early peoples who decided the fate of a condemned criminal by means of a gamble. They allowed a person who had been sentenced to death to "choose" the time of execution by shooting an arrow into a grove of trees. The backs of the trees were marked with different dates. The tree struck determined the date on which the criminal would die.

Sometime between the first and fifth centuries A.D., Phoenician and Arab seamen made their way to the islands off the eastern coast of Africa, one of them probably being Zanzibar. They found the people of the islands playing a game in which stones were moved about in an area of sand. The idea was to be the first player to reach a prize—perhaps a trinket or some household item—at the center of the area. Today the Arabian people in Africa still play and wager on an ancient game in the sand. Stones are used in the game, which is called dara and is similar to our tic-tac-toe.

A game that may have been the great-grandfather of chess was being played in China some 2,300 years ago. Known as wei-ch'i, it was a war game in which the players maneuvered hundreds of pieces, representing soldiers and equipment, about a large board. According to early Chinese writings, it was invented by the Emperor Yao to help sharpen his son's mind.

Many of the games that first appeared in distant parts of the world were eventually played in Europe. Some may have been carried by travelers or foreign visitors. Some—by coincidence or perhaps because human beings in widely separated regions often create the same things—may have been invented there. One of the last arrivals in Europe was card playing, which initially appeared sometime in the 1300s. Some historians think that the people who fought in the series of holy wars called the Crusades probably brought back the cards they had come across in the Middle East. It is also possible that the cards were carried along by invaders from Mongolia.

Whatever the origin, Europeans were enthusiastic gamblers and quickly adopted card playing. In the next centuries it became one of the most popular pastimes on the Continent, followed closely by dice and roulette, a French invention of the 1600s that may have been based on an old Chinese game. During those centuries, the Europeans invented a host of games for gambling or entertainment purposes. Among them were games that are popular to this day in Europe, the United States, and many other parts of the world—poker, blackjack, rummy, and whist.

In all, hundreds of games that could be played

for gambling or entertainment were developed through the ages. But no matter where or how they were played, they all fell into three general categories:

♥ *Games of chance:* These games require no playing skills, with chance controlling all. They include lotteries, bingo, and most dice games.

♠ *Games of skill:* The element of chance plays little or no part in these games. Success depends on a player's skill. Examples include chess and checkers.

♦ *Games that combine chance and skill:* Most card games involve chance (the cards that are dealt to a player) and then the skill that enables the player to play wisely. Sports betting is also a chance-skill activity. A player can skillfully bet on football games, for instance, by studying the team records, only to have chance take over—perhaps an injury to a star player—and lead to a loss.

European gambling was carried across the Atlantic Ocean to the New World with the early settlers. It was joined with the games of chance and skill that American Indians had played for ages. We'll turn to the history of gambling in the United States in the next chapter.

♣ CENTURIES OF CRITICISM

To say that the passing centuries have seen people everywhere risking anything from pennies to fortunes on bets is to tell only one side of the gambling story. For perhaps as long as it has been around, gambling has been roundly denounced and criticized for a variety of reasons[3] stemming from moral, social, economic, or personal beliefs.

Almost all religions have moral objections to gambling. For example, there is the prohibition found in the Koran, the holy book of Islam. It forbids Muslim people to gamble because it wastes time and takes their minds away from "remembering God and prayer." Muslims believe the Koran is made up of the words of God as passed on to the founder of Islam, Muhammad, in the seventh century A.D.

Many Christians have opposed gambling. Saint Luke wrote some twenty centuries ago: "Even the hairs on your head are numbered." The meaning of his statement is that everything in the world is ruled by God and subject at all times to God's laws. As a result, there is no such thing as chance. But gambling is always a matter of chance, and so it conflicts with a belief in God. In effect, it denies God's existence and is consequently immoral.

Despite this belief, countless Christians gamble, and their churches regard gambling with different degrees of concern. Among some fundamentalist faiths, gambling is condemned as "the devil's work," a phrase used long ago in both Europe and America. The Roman Catholic church, however, has generally looked on gambling as a deeply rooted part of human life and thus views it with tolerance. Nevertheless, Catholicism and other faiths are concerned with the social harm that gambling can do—how it can, for example, turn players into addicts or cause them to forget that honest work, not luck, brings the worthwhile things in life.

These same social concerns were felt in ancient times by the Greek philosopher Aristotle (384–322 B.C.). When writing of what he had seen of gambling, Aristotle charged it with triggering avarice and the urge to cheat.

The ancient Jews felt that gambling weakened their society and threatened their legal system. Consequently, they barred known gamblers from participating in trials as lawyers, judges, and witnesses.

Their belief was that debt-ridden gamblers might accept bribes from one side or the other.

Both the Greeks and the Romans also viewed gambling as a threat to the well-being of their societies. It wasted the time of the people and took their minds off their work. It also tempted public officials to steal from the state coffers to pay their gambling debts. Both cultures established laws to discourage play. A Roman measure stipulated that winners could not collect their winnings and that losers need not pay their debts.

As we saw in Chapter 1 and will see again in later chapters, the opinion that gambling is a threat to society continues to be held in modern times.

Two European kings of the twelfth century A.D. took action when they became convinced that gambling was harming their realms. So much playing was going on that Richard the Lion-Hearted of England and Philip II of France decided that their people were devoting far too little time to the daily work needed for the advancement of the two countries. And so they enacted laws that stipulated who could and who could not gamble.

An odd view that many people in the past held toward gambling can be seen in these laws. Neither of those two kings placed himself on the list of people not permitted to gamble. This was a reflection of a snobbish attitude that dated back to the ancient Egyptians and their idea that gambling was a pleasure. As such, it was fit only for the wealthy and noble. It had no place among the poor, who were fated to work hard for a living.

Much the same view was held in Rome. The many laws against gambling were aimed at keeping the working people from wasting their time and were ignored by the wealthy and the noble. In all, gambling was considered an activity for the privileged classes. No one said a thing—at least not out loud—when the news went around that the emperor Nero was in the habit of betting the equivalent of $50,000 on a single chariot race. Nor was a word said when it became known that the mad emperor Caligula (A.D. 12–41) paid his gambling debts by dreaming up criminal charges against his wealthiest citizens, imprisoning them, and then seizing their riches.

The idea that gambling belonged to the privileged was seen in British law for some three centuries. Between 1661 and 1960 Britain enacted measures that suppressed many forms of gambling. The prohibitions mainly affected the poor while the rich were able to bet openly on horse races and various games. Illegal play, however, flourished, as has so often been the case when gambling has been driven underground. In 1960 the British began to drop their restrictions of old. Today all types of gambling are legally available in Great Britain.

There was also the feeling in many societies that the poor had to be protected against the risk of gambling away what little money they had. This same view is voiced today by some people who oppose legal gambling in the United States. It is aimed in particular at the state lotteries.

From the earliest of times on, many people have personally objected to gambling because of the outrageous things it drove some players to do. The history of gambling abounds with stories of foolish, dangerous, and cruel bets. Here are just three examples that demonstrate how bad things got at times.

To begin, there is a Chinese poem about two men who made a bet on which of its sides a birch leaf would land when it fell from a tree. The stakes: their ears. Honoring the wager, the loser immediately cut off his ears and handed them to his fellow gambler. The poem was written in the fourth century B.C.

Next comes the account that the Greek philosopher and biographer, Plutarch (c. 46–c. 120 A.D.), wrote of one of the cruelest wagers on record. He described how a queen of Persia gambled with a friend for the life of a slave. On winning, she had the slave tortured and put to death.

And finally there is the story of what may well be the silliest bet in history. It comes from the time when the Goths, a people from northern Europe, were invading Roman territory in the third century A.D. and tells of what happened when a band of the invaders stumbled upon a Roman troop. A sharp battle ensued, with the Goths proving victorious. But they were avid gamblers who, for some reason, loved to take nonsensical risks. And so they challenged the defeated Romans to a wager: A flip of a coin would determine which side would become the other's prisoner. The Goths lost. Without complaint, they allowed themselves to be taken prisoner by the men they had bested in battle.

GAMBLING IN THE UNITED STATES

European gambling traveled westward across the Atlantic Ocean with Christopher Columbus in 1492. The men who sailed aboard the *Nina*, the *Pinta*, and the *Santa Maria* carried packs of cards to pass the off-duty hours at sea. However, when the three ships had been out of sight of land for long weeks, the crewmen became frightened by the thought that they might never see home again. In common with sea-farers throughout the ages, they were a superstitious lot. Somehow they took it into their heads that their cards were bringing them bad luck. And so, over the sides went the packs. A short time later a smudge of land appeared on the horizon at the edge of what was soon to be called the New World.

The crewmen quickly returned to their old gambling ways. Wherever they went ashore in the next weeks, they fashioned cards for themselves, usually from the leaves of native plants. The Native Americans who came out to meet them watched all this activity with interest and began to join the newcomers in their play. It took the crewmen no time to realize that the New World Indians were enthusiastic gamblers.[1]

♥ GAMBLING IN COLONIAL AMERICA

All the explorers and settlers who came in the wake of Columbus saw that same enthusiasm wherever they went in the New World.[2] When the British and Dutch arrived in what is now New York State, they found the Iroquois Indians playing a game with dice made of peach and plum stones. Some miles to the north, the Narragansets had dice games in which entire villages noisily participated. Other tribes wagered on the spins of a crude wheel or, as Leif Ericson had seen in Nova Scotia centuries earlier, a stick. Wherever the newcomers went as later exploration and settlement took them farther and farther west, they saw much gambling among the native tribes, with favorites for betting being footraces, jumping contests, and target events with knives, spears, and bows and arrows.

Some pretty heavy wagering took place between the newcomers and the American Indians. The early Spanish explorers, for instance, played cards with the tribes they met and then saw them make their own cards of sheepskin and deerskin. The settlers at England's first New World colony—tiny Jamestown—learned to gamble on native games and soon had the surrounding Indians betting on such European favorites as cockfighting and horse racing.

Jamestown was not only the scene of gambling between the settlers and the Indians but also owed its survival to some gambling that was done back in England. The colony was first established in 1607, with such hard times then following that its people were ready to abandon the place and head home in

1612. But a lottery was held in England that year, and the proceeds were spent on outfitting two ships to sail to Virginia with supplies and new settlers. Once they arrived there, Jamestown began to thrive and was never again in danger of desertion.

It would be a mistake, however, to think that all the early European settlers gambled. Many looked on gambling as a vice and had little or no time for it, being far too busy trying to make a life for themselves in the wilderness. But there was enough play going on with the American Indians and between the colonists themselves to upset the leaders of the settlements. In Virginia, the amount of wagering, the drinking that went with it, and the time it wasted were such that the colony's governing body took action. Passed into law in 1624 was a measure that was aimed at the local clergy. It dictated that "Mynisters shall not give themselfes to excesse in drinking and yette spend their time idelie by day or night, playing at dice, cards, or any unlawfull game."

Obviously the gambling ways of some of the clergy were not helping them to serve as models of proper behavior for the people.

Also worried were the leaders of New England's Plymouth Colony. The colony had been settled by Puritans, many of whom abhorred gambling as the "Devil's work." But regardless of this outlook, so much attention was being given to card games that the leaders passed an anti-gambling law in 1656. They set a fine of forty shillings for anyone caught playing with what they called the "Devil's Picture Books." In addition to the fine, children who violated the law were to be punished by their parents, and servants by their masters. A second offense called for a guilty adult player "to bee publickly whipt."

The leaders of the Dutch settlement at New Amsterdam also found gambling a headache. At the time the Plymouth Colony passed its anti-gambling law, the Dutch enacted one of their own. It prohibited the playing of tric-trac during church services. Tric-trac is the French name for backgammon, a game that can be traced back to ancient times. (Backgammon is a "race" between two players along a playing board, with their moves determined by dice throws.)

♠ GAMBLING IN THE YOUNG UNITED STATES

Gambling played a role not only in the early exploration and settlement of North America but also in the birth of the United States.[3] In 1777, just months after the American colonies declared their independence from Great Britain, the Continental Congress set out to provide funds for the American troops by holding a lottery. The commander of the new Yankee force, General George Washington, purchased the first ticket.

The aim of the lottery was to raise $10 million for the army. However, slow ticket sales (the people did not think the new government's money would be worth anything) and a number of other problems soon caused the sponsors to call the whole thing off. The army was then financed with taxes. Later financial help came from France.

A number of the nation's founding fathers liked to gamble. Among them were George Washington, Thomas Jefferson, and Benjamin Franklin. Washington enjoyed card games and passed some of the nights during the terrible winter at Valley Forge playing them. Both Jefferson and his wife played backgammon for money. It is also known that Jefferson spent his evenings testing his luck at a form of poker while he was writing the Declaration of Independence.

The man who was to become the nation's third president may have enjoyed cards and backgammon, but he detested the idea of gambling. Jefferson once wrote that it "corrupts our dispositions and teaches the habit of hostility against all mankind."

Benjamin Franklin often played cribbage with his wife. In 1748, long before he helped to found the United States, Franklin assisted in organizing a lottery to provide arms with which to protect the city of Philadelphia from attack during the French and Indian War.

Gambling continued to be a part of the infant nation's daily life as explorers, traders, and settlers moved westward from the Atlantic coast to the continent's midsection. By the early 1800s, the banks of the Mississippi River were well settled and marked all along their length with towns and ports, chief among them Cincinnati, Ohio; Memphis, Tennessee; St. Louis, Missouri; and New Orleans, Louisiana. Connecting the towns and turning the river into a miles-long gambling hall was a fleet of paddle-wheel steamboats.

The first steamboat appeared on the Mississippi in 1811. By 1820 the river was home for sixty paddle wheelers. The next thirteen years brought their number to five hundred. Daily they carried merchandise and passengers from port to port.

From the 1830s onward, about 1,500 professional gamblers worked the steamboats. With card and dice games, they relieved the monotony of the river ride for the passengers, many of whom were planters whose pockets were well lined with cash. Some of the professionals were honest players whose wins depended on luck and skill. But far too many were dishonest and known as cardsharps. They brought loaded dice, marked cards, and other forms of trickery to the table. (Marked cards, as their name indicates, have tiny markings on their backs that reveal the value of any card held by the cheat's opponents.)

A favorite trick of many cardsharps was never to let it be known that they were professionals. Rather, they passed themselves off as innocent passengers, usually posing as merchants, farmers, planters, or naive country bumpkins. They customarily worked in teams, with the members pretending not to know one another.

Their next trick was to set upon their prey in the following manner. One team member would engage a passenger or two in conversation and eventually suggest a friendly game of poker. The accomplices would then appear and ask if they might join the game and fill up the rest of the seats at the table. Within the next few hours, the duped passenger would be poorer by several hundred dollars.

But what if a sharp found himself in a game with experienced players? Now he could not depend on his teammates or on tricks like marked cards to win. And so, pretending to be casual spectators, his accomplices would gather about the table and quietly signal to him the cards held by his opponents.

A number of cardsharps made a specialty of signaling. One of the most unusual was a man named James Ashby. He disguised himself as a tattered and half-mad violinist who strolled among the tables, subjected the passengers to wild talk, and now and again scratched out tunes on his violin. What no one—except his teammates—knew was that his tunes were signals telling them what cards their opponents held.

Though Ashby was one of the most unusual figures of the period, he is today one of the least known.

Far more famous are two lawmen who participated in the nation's advance into the Far West and who, thanks to television and motion pictures, remain with us as folk heroes—Wyatt Earp and Wild Bill Hickok. Both were gamblers as well as lawmen. Earp was a professional; Hickok, though not a professional, was an avid poker player.

In the late 1800s, Wyatt Earp (1848–1929) served as U.S. marshal at several towns, chief among them Dodge City, Kansas, and Tombstone, Arizona. But while on duty at Tombstone, he owned a part interest in a casino called the Oriental Saloon and Gambling House. He dealt card games there and is said to have made more money as a dealer than as a lawman. It was during his Tombstone years that he won lasting fame for his role in the 1881 gunfight at the O.K. Corral.

William "Wild Bill" Hickok (1837–1876), who got his nickname from his steely eyes and his adventurous ways, served as a Union sharpshooter, scout, and spy in the Civil War. He then worked as a U.S. marshal for several years in three of the wildest towns that Kansas had to offer—Fort Riley, Hays, and Abilene—where he proved to be a dedicated lawman who relentlessly tracked down outlaws and recovered hundreds of stolen horses, mules, and cattle. He met his death on August 2, 1876, while playing poker in a saloon at the town of Deadwood in the Dakota Territory. The story of his death is one of the most famous in the history of the West.

When Hickok settled down to play that day, he broke an old rule. He had always insisted on sitting with his back to a wall so that he could have a view of the room and be able to see any enemy who came through the front door. But no such seat was available and so the rule went ignored. This enabled a man named Jack McCall to enter the saloon, walk up behind Hickok, and shoot him in the back of the head. It was later learned that a group of gamblers in Deadwood had hired McCall to kill Hickok. They feared that Hickok was about to be appointed the local marshal. They knew that, if given the job, he would crack down as hard on them as he had on the outlaws in other towns.

At the moment of his death Hickok had just drawn a hand that included two aces and two eights—all in black suits. Ever since, the combination of a pair of aces and a pair of eights has been known to poker players as a "dead man's hand."

♦ A GAMBLING FEVER

While there had been gambling before and immediately after the birth of the United States, it was little compared to the amount of play that went on during the westward expansion of the 1800s. Critics of the time—sounding exactly like the critics of today—charged that the young nation was in the grip of a gambling fever.[4]

A number of factors accounted for the excessive play. For one, the many hardworking people who moved westward to and beyond the Mississippi for the purpose of establishing farms, ranches, and businesses were joined by thousands of a less responsible nature. There were adventurers in search of quick riches, drifters without any aim in life, escapees from the police back home, and prospectors looking for silver in Nevada and gold in California and Colorado. They were all willing to take the risk of venturing into wild country, and that willingness extended itself to taking risks at the gambling tables. Along with them came the professional players, the cheats, and the gambling hall operators, all ready to separate them from their money.

Further, much of the land along the Mississippi and virtually all of it to the west was still open and untamed. Most of the towns that took shape were without laws to control gambling. In those towns that managed to establish such laws, the police—sometimes no more than a sheriff or a marshal and a deputy or two—were often helpless to stop the play. Larger police forces were likely to be paid by the gambling interests to look the other way.

Finally, out at the edge of the ever-advancing frontier, the towns were so small or so remote that gambling and the drinking that invariably went with it were the only forms of entertainment at hand.

Consequently, wherever towns sprouted and blossomed into cities, gambling flowered with them. New Orleans, which had been founded by the French in 1718, was so famous for its many casinos in the early 1800s that it became known as America's first great gambling center. But there was such rowdyism, drunkenness, and cheating in some of the places that the Louisiana legislature finally cracked down on them in 1832 with a law that banned gambling statewide. But illegal play then flourished in the city for years to come.

Far to the west, the California gold rush of 1849 turned San Francisco from a sleepy village into a boomtown. The city served as the arrival point for adventurers pouring in from all parts of the world in search of quick riches in the Sierra Nevada. It greeted them with a clutter of flimsy tent-and-board hotels, restaurants, and gambling halls, all carelessly and quickly nailed up. San Francisco's downtown district burned to the ground six times between 1849 and 1852. Local lore holds that some of the fires were started accidentally by drunken miners—or deliberately by angry losers—when they knocked over oil lamps and set the makeshift gambling halls ablaze.

Chicago's great fire of 1871, which destroyed the city, may also have been the result of a gambling accident. It was long believed that the blaze erupted when a cow belonging to a Mrs. O'Leary kicked over a lantern and set fire to a pile of hay while being milked. But a local businessman, upon his death in 1944, left a gift of $35,000 to Northwestern University, along with an explanation of how the fire actually started. He claimed that, as a youth, he had accidentally kicked over an oil lamp during an exciting moment in a dice game.

Had you been alive in the 1800s, you would have found gambling in practically every town you visited. You would have learned that Cincinnati's love of card playing earned it the nickname "Pokeropolis." In Dodge City you would have found that the wagering and drinking there had caused one visitor to describe the town as "the wickedest and most bibulous Babylon on the frontier." Arriving in Kansas City you would have come upon forty gambling halls, all doing a roaring business. Then, in Abilene, you would have counted twenty gambling halls waiting for the arrival of the cattle drivers up from Texas. Down in Texas itself you might have happened on the tiny town where a visiting journalist said he often saw a hundred thousand dollars change hands in a single night of card playing.

But, had you lived in the 1890s, you would have seen a growing public disgust at the amount of gambling in the country and the trouble it was causing. You would have seen states everywhere begin to outlaw it in all its forms. Further, in 1894, you would have seen Congress ban lotteries nationwide. By the dawn of the twentieth century, only a handful of states allowed horse racing, and only in Nevada was casino gambling permitted. Then, in 1911, even Nevada did away with casino play.

Though driven underground and made illegal,

gambling went right on flourishing—in back-alley dice games, in clandestine sports betting, and in casinos that city police and politicians were paid to ignore. Millions of dollars continued to change hands across the country.

In 1931 Nevada reinstated casino gambling because the state was caught in the Great Depression and was hard-pressed for the money it needed to survive. The gambling halls there were small places during the 1930s. In the 1940s, though the state had such reputable casino owners as William Harrah and Harold Smith, some of the Nevada casinos, especially those in Las Vegas, were in the hands of underworld figures, who built large operations with hotels attached. But over the years and particularly in the 1960s the underworld owners were bought out and replaced by reputable operators, chief among them Howard Hughes. Casino gambling in Nevada gradually earned a reputation of respectability and of being well controlled by the state. Today many Nevada casinos are owned by such respected corporations as the Hilton Hotel chain.

In the 1970s and 1980s legal gambling reappeared across the nation as numerous states established lotteries to raise public funds and as New Jersey authorized casino play and Iowa permitted riverboat gambling on the Mississippi. At present, forty-eight of our fifty states allow some form of gambling. Only in Utah and Hawaii, as mentioned earlier, is gambling still prohibited.

♣ GAMBLING IN AMERICA TODAY

Today legal gambling is recognized as one of the nation's largest and fastest-growing industries.[5] Just how large is it? In the 1990s it is bringing in well over $250 billion a year, more than twice the amount garnered by the nation's largest corporation, General Motors. Of that total, more than $196 billion is being reaped from casino play. The state lotteries are grossing over $19.5 billion. Horse and dog racing are bringing in around $17.5 billion. Last in line is sports betting, on football and other games, with around $2 billion.

And just how fast is the gambling industry growing? A comparison of present-day earnings with those of recent years gives us the answer. In 1987, for example, the nation's casinos brought in $145 billion—some $51 billion less than today's figure. The state lotteries in 1982 grossed $4.1 million—about 20 percent of their current gross. That same year horse and dog racing brought in $14.5 billion—$3 billion below their present take.

Added to the earnings reaped from legal gambling are those brought in by illegal gambling. The total amount of money spent on illegal play is, of course, unknown. But it is estimated to run from $30 billion up to $42 billion a year. Altogether, gambling in the United States, both legal and illegal, harvests between $282 billion and $294 billion annually.

In 1990 Philip G. Satre, the president and chief executive officer of Harrah's Hotels and Casinos in Nevada, predicted that by the year 2000, all forms of gambling—both legal and illegal—will be bringing in over $500 billion a year. Mr. Satre made his prediction in a speech on the state of U.S. gambling to the Commonwealth Club of California.

If his prediction is on the mark, we can expect the number of Americans who try their hand at gambling to grow steadily in the next years. Among them will be an increasing number of the country's young people. And among those young people will be a growing number who join those who already suffer the tragedy of being compulsive gamblers.

THE COMPULSIVE GAMBLER

Current estimates hold that there are from 8 to 10 million compulsive gamblers in the United States. Of that number, approximately 1 million are said to be in their teens.

In this chapter and those that follow we will look at compulsive gamblers and the varied problems they suffer. We'll do this by pretending that you yourself are—or are becoming—a compulsive gambler so that your look can be an especially personal one.

Most of the research to date on compulsive gambling has been done with adults. Consequently, much of what we have to say will concern grown players. But it is material of importance to you if you are presently developing a strong gambling habit. This is because either of two fates may lurk in your future. You may become a compulsive while still young, or it may happen later on, in adulthood. You need to know what lies ahead in each case.

Studies made in recent years indicate that the majority of adult compulsive gamblers got their start in their youth or childhood. One study, for instance, asked thirty-five adult compulsives when they first began to gamble. The average age they gave was thirteen. Almost half said they had begun somewhere between age eleven and nineteen. Thirty-seven percent reported starting before age ten. Only 14 percent said they had started after age nineteen.[1]

♥ WHO ARE THE COMPULSIVE GAMBLERS?

Today you and your companion compulsive gamblers come from all walks of life, are of both sexes, and range in age from the early teens to the seventies and eighties.[2] This was not the case twenty years ago. Surveys of the people who joined Gamblers Anonymous at that time in an effort to end their problem showed the typical compulsive player to be a white middle-class, middle-aged man.

But all that has changed as the appeal of gambling has spread across the country in the years since. Dr. Valerie C. Lorenz, executive director of the Center for Pathological Gambling (a national organization dedicated to the treatment of compulsive gamblers and to education and research in compulsive gambling), says that compulsive gambling has become "democratic," meaning that it has caught every type of person in its web. When appearing recently on a television documentary, "Your Lucky Number," she remarked that the ranks of the compulsives today are filled with all types of people—men, women, blacks, whites, housewives, and professional workers. In her view, gambling has indeed become democratic.

Giving substance to Dr. Lorenz's remark is a statement in *Final Report: Task Force on Gambling Addiction in Maryland:* "Today, a compulsive gambler may be a teenager or a retired senior citizen, male or female, a businessman, blue collar or white collar worker, military member, student or house-wife." Further, the report states that the compulsive can be found at any level of society, can be "highly educated or illiterate," can belong to "any racial or ethnic group," or be of "any religious inclination." In short, virtually every type of person can be found alongside you in the ranks of the compulsive gamblers.

(The Task Force was formed in 1988 to learn if compulsive gambling constitutes a health problem in Maryland. With a membership made up of researchers, legislators, reporters, interested citizens, and providers of treatment for gambling problems, the task force worked throughout 1989 and published its final report in 1990. The report pointed out that compulsive gambling is indeed a costly health problem for the state and requires educational and treatment programs to alleviate it. Dr. Lorenz and Dr. Robert M. Politzer, the director of research for the Washington Center for Pathological Gambling, served as co-chairpersons for the group.)

Though compulsive gamblers are now of all ages and found in all walks of life, males dominate their ranks. Indications of the preponderance of males can be clearly seen in the annual reports from the telephone hot lines that the states of New Jersey and Maryland operate for compulsives seeking help to end their problem. Both hot lines handle thousands of calls annually from inside and outside their state boundaries; the Maryland line alone received almost 12,000 calls during its 1990 fiscal year. In 1989 the New Jersey line reported that 82 percent of its calls for help came from males and 18 percent from females that year. The Maryland line reported that, in 1990, males accounted for 81 percent of its calls, with 19 percent coming from females.

Females may be in the minority among compulsives, but their number is rapidly swelling. In a 1990 issue of the *Journal of Gambling Studies* (formerly the *Journal of Gambling Behavior*), Dr. Lorenz writes that, as recently as ten years ago, female compulsives were rarities in treatment programs but that now they are found everywhere, at Gamblers Anonymous meetings and in various treatment and rehabilitation programs. Today, though the estimates of their number vary, there are assuredly more women compulsive gamblers than ever before in the nation's history. Some researchers believe that one out of every ten compulsives is a woman. The Task Force studying gambling addiction in Maryland believes the number is far higher—one out of every four.

An additional report from the New Jersey hot line gives a solid example of the increase in female compulsives. Their calls to the hot line from mid-1987 to mid-1988 jumped by 140 percent over preceding years.

And what of young people such as yourself? In her article for the *Journal of Gambling Studies*, Dr. Lorenz says that teenage compulsives were nonexistent in treatment programs ten or so years ago. But now, along with women, you and other young people everywhere are seeking help for your problem. As stated in Chapter 1, counselors today claim that about 7 percent of their cases involve teenagers with gambling problems.

You are, however, still in a minority when compared to adults. The Maryland hot line reports that in 1990 only 2 percent of its calls from both inside and outside the state came from teenagers. But your calls are on the increase. In 1991 they doubled—to 4 percent.

There will be more information on the Maryland

hot line and others in a later chapter so that you can reach them if you need to.

♠ COMPULSIVE GAMBLING: AN ILLNESS

There was a time when you, as a compulsive gambler, would have been automatically branded as a weak or bad person who suffered a character flaw that not only made you gamble in the first place but also caused you to gamble compulsively. This attitude has been changing in recent years as research has told us more and more about your problem and the forces that lead to it. Today, though many people continue to regard your habit as a sign of "badness" or weakness, compulsive gambling is widely seen as an illness.[3]

Dr. Robert Custer, in his 1985 book, *When Luck Runs Out: Help for Compulsive Gamblers and Their Families* (written with Harry Milt, the author of several books on mental health problems), says that we can thank psychiatrists and psychologists for this change of attitude. He writes that, just a few decades ago, "the term 'illness' or 'disease' was automatically taken to mean something physically wrong with a person." But now, due to the work done over the years in the mental health field, we have come to recognize that there are illnesses that are not physical in nature. They are psychological illnesses—illnesses such as depression and phobias. They can arise from psychological stresses that a person has suffered in the past or is suffering now. Compulsive gambling is included among their number.

But what, exactly, is this illness that you suffer? An answer comes from Dr. Custer in *When Luck Runs Out*. He describes compulsive gambling as an addictive illness, meaning that, once you become its victim, you are driven by an "overwhelming uncontrollable impulse" to continue gambling. This impulse grows steadily, eating up more and more of your time, your energy, your emotions, and your material wealth. Finally it invades all corners of your life, often damaging and even destroying everything that has meaning to you.

(Dr. Custer is a psychiatrist who has long specialized in helping compulsive gamblers overcome their problem. In 1972, at Brecksville, Ohio, he founded the nation's first treatment center for compulsive gamblers. He is now the consulting medical director for the Compulsive Gambling Program at Charter Hospital in Las Vegas, Nevada.)

The addictive illness that is compulsive gambling can begin in any number of ways. Perhaps, in your life, it starts when you receive your first invitation to join a card game for fun; perhaps when you innocently buy your first lottery ticket; or perhaps when you try your hand at gambling because you think it interesting and have always been attracted to it. Whatever the case, your first gambling experience may give you a feeling of pleasure or enable you to escape for a while from the pain of some emotional or mental upset that you've suffered in the past or are now suffering. For example, hear what two adult compulsives remember of their first teenage gambling experience:

Dan

I was seventeen when I got into a poker game with some guys after school. Something really great happened. I didn't know much about poker, but I hit it lucky and won a lot. The guys with me were really impressed. I forgot that I wasn't much liked at school and that I had a face full of pimples.

Martha

My husband and I were married when we had just turned eighteen. We were both too young, and we both had rotten tempers. We were always fighting, and I just had to get out of the house. Betting on the horses was the perfect way to get out and to forget everything that was wrong in my life.

If your first gambling session brings you a sense of pleasure or escape, you may want to relive the experience, and you will go on gambling. The same thing will happen if you do not have the ability or the chance to find that pleasure or escape in some other pursuit.

Should you continue to gamble for a long period, a psychological change occurs in you. You begin to crave gambling. You eventually develop what is called a *psychic dependence* on it, meaning that you feel you *must* gamble to find whatever pleasure or escape it is that you are seeking; without it, you are unhappy, angry, tense, distraught. In time, you join the ranks of the compulsives. You need to gamble again and again—most likely every day—and are willing to do anything to raise the money for your next bet.

But there is a mystery here. Millions of people gamble, many of them quite regularly. Yet they never become compulsives, while you and many others do. Why? Why do some avoid addiction, no matter how often or how regularly they play? Why do you and others lose control and become addicts, desiring above all else to experience a certain pleasure time and again, even long after your addiction has made gambling no longer a pleasure? Dr. Custer writes that no one yet knows the answer. He hopes that present and future research into the problem will one day show us the answer.

He and other experts on compulsive gambling,

however, have some strong suspicions as to why you lose control. Their suspicions are based on what they have seen of the personalities of the compulsives with whom they've dealt.

◆ YOU AS A COMPULSIVE GAMBLER

Research into gambling shows that you and your fellow compulsives are usually blessed with some very positive, enviable personality traits.[4] The members of the Maryland Task Force, for example have this to say about you in their *Final Report:* "The pathological [compulsive] gambler can be described as an individual who is above average in intelligence, honest, energetic, competitive, creative, hardworking and motivated to achieve."

This same view is voiced, in much the same language, by Dr. Custer. In *When Luck Runs Out*, he writes that most compulsive gamblers are blessed by nature with a superior intelligence, an eagerness to get ahead, and a boundless capacity for hard work. They are likewise, he contends, blessed with great energy, physical stamina, and emotional endurance.

To substantiate his views, the doctor quotes comments made about themselves by a number of compulsives under his care. The statements leave little doubt about the speakers' intelligence, energy, and willingness to work. Here are just two:

> I worked in a warehouse after school every year I attended high school. Weekends I caddied at the country club. My schoolwork did not suffer.

> My parents couldn't afford to send me to law school so I had to support myself and pay tuition. I went to law school days, on a regular program, and worked full-time as a copy editor on a newspaper in the evening.

Dr. Custer then adds these details to the portrait of your personality: Though some of your number are loners, you are most likely friendly and sociable. You are also very generous—sometimes, the doctor thinks, to a fault. Your friendliness, sociability, and fine intelligence endow you with strong powers of persuasion and leadership. In addition, you love stimulation, excitement, and change. You feel the same way about risk, challenge, and change.

Many of these characteristics are shared by people who never gamble or who gamble, sometimes quite regularly, without ever becoming compulsives. What makes you different from them?

In answer, Dr. Custer turns to the darker side of your nature. He says that, while you are sometimes friendly and sociable, you are not always this way; you can also be sullen, irritable, and withdrawn. He feels that your sociability and friendliness often mask low self-esteem—the deep and nagging feeling that you are not the person you should be and that you are not liked or approved of by the people around you. Your generosity is often the tool you use to win friends and keep them beholden to you. It's a way of helping you to convince yourself that you're better than you think you are.

But what of your powers of persuasion and leadership? The doctor believes these powers may well be a facade covering an ego made shaky and insecure by your low self-esteem.

And your devotion to hard work? This may be another desperate effort to bolster your ego, this time by acquiring the material symbols of success and the respect you feel they will bring you.

Next, your competitive drive: It's likely powered by a desire to erase the poor image you have of yourself. Many people like to compete in games for the fun of it, but Dr. Custer says that the compulsive gambler *needs* to compete. "When he wins and comes out on top, he is able to say to himself, and to everyone else, 'Look how important I am.' " One of the doctor's patients has this to say about his early years:

> I was wound up like a spring. I had to get into everything where there was a chance to compete—track, swimming, baseball. Part of it was the excitement of competing, of matching myself up against the others and giving everything I had to beat them. But winning, that was the thing, to hear the crowd yell my name, hear the applause and the cheering. It was like drinking champagne.

Now, your love of stimulation, excitement, and change: Many people like these same things, but your feelings for them go far beyond even love. Your nature makes you *crave* them, and where better to find them than in gambling? Dr. Custer remarks that compulsives are restless and hyperactive individuals. They have trouble with quiet pursuits that require time and patience, become easily bored, and need to be constantly on the move.

These traits, he explains, do not suddenly emerge in adulthood. They are present in childhood and are seen, for example, in unruly classroom behavior, the inability to concentrate on quiet school subjects, and the tendency to become quickly tired of friends and drop them for new acquaintances. He remarks that such youngsters often begin experimenting with sex, alcohol, drugs, and gambling long before others in their age group.

Finally, your love of risk, challenge, and adventure: Of these traits, Dr. Custer writes:

> The essence of gambling is risk. For many people that is the reason *not* to gamble; they would rather hold on to

what they've got or put it into something safe. For the person who becomes a compulsive gambler it is the other way around. It is the risk that attracts him—pitting himself against the odds, against chance, against the operators of the game—as well as the prize that awaits him should he win. . . .

Risk, challenge, adventure—that is what these people thrive on long before they go into serious gambling. They are dating and making sexual conquests while others are still going through their first timid approaches. . . . Sports draw them like magnets, not only because of the competition but also because of the challenge to their strength, skill, and agility. . . . They love to put themselves on the line in win-lose situations."

When a friend who is a recovering compulsive was asked the reason for this love, he shrugged and said, "I guess it's just in our nature." Then, after a moment's thought, he added, "But there are some other things. I think you're trying to prove something to yourself—maybe that you're better than you really are just because you've got the guts to go up against some cardplayers or a dealer in a casino. If you win, I'll tell you for sure that you really feel good. Really important and sharp. A winner. But if you lose, it hurts—but it doesn't stop you from wanting more of the excitement and wanting to win."

In total, Dr. Custer sees compulsives as lonely, insecure people with shaky egos and low self-esteem. They are gambling, he writes, in a desperate effort to (1) overcome their loneliness, (2) avoid rejection, (3) acquire the possessions and position that will win them recognition and approval, and (4) demonstrate the strength and power that will prove to themselves that they are not helpless victims in life.

Of the above points, the desire to gain possessions and to demonstrate power and strength seems to be found more in the male compulsive than in the female. The same holds true for the wish to experience the excitement of gambling play. In a recent study of fifty women members of Gamblers Anonymous, Dr. Henry R. Lesieur of Saint John's University in Jamaica, New York, concluded that most women compulsives begin their gambling in an effort to escape a problem in life. For example, some may be trying to run from the memories of an unhappy childhood or an overly strict upbringing. Some may be trying, as Martha did, to escape an unhappy marriage.

Now we come to the question of how you and your fellow compulsives developed the shaky egos and low self-esteem that have put you in such danger. The members of the Task Force on Gambling Addiction in Maryland offer some answers. In their final report they write of the problems that many compulsives face in childhood.

For one, there is almost always some serious emotional disorder in the family. The parents may have a history of fighting, alcoholism, or drug abuse. Factors such as these can damage any child's view of himself or herself; many youngsters, too young to know better, blame themselves for the family troubles. The parents may also be pathological gamblers, with the child then taking up gambling because it has always been a normal way of family life.

Examples of the problems that can be suffered in childhood are seen in the results of the Lesieur study of fifty women compulsives. Though some of the women claimed to have enjoyed happy lives as children, most talked of having to endure some sort of unhappiness. Fourteen spoke of alcoholic fathers, and five mentioned alcoholic mothers. Seven said their fathers were compulsive gamblers; two leveled the same charge against their mothers. Six talked of parents with mental or emotional problems; one woman said her father had once been hospitalized as a manic-depressive.

Turning to another problem, the Maryland Task Force says that the compulsive gambler is typically raised in a family in which much emphasis is placed on money and its importance. Taught that money is so important, the compulsive is hooked on gambling for the same reason that he or she is such a hard worker—to garner the wealth that will enhance his or her standing in the eyes of the surrounding world.

Still another problem: The Task Force members point out that the compulsive often suffers physical and/or verbal abuse as a child. It is obvious what such abuse will do to one's self-esteem. Again, specific examples of the suffering endured come from Dr. Lesieur's study. Of the fifty women he interviewed, two said they had been sexually abused by their fathers. Several admitted to sexual, physical, or emotional abuse by their stepfathers or their mothers' boyfriends, some of whom were alcoholics or drug users. To escape the problems at home, four had run away in their youth and several said they had married early.

The Task Force members further report that various other problems also mar many a compulsive's childhood. There is, for instance, parental separation through death or divorce. Or the death of a brother or sister. Afraid to talk of their anguish over these losses because of the pain and grief it will trigger, the child and the family may be unable to face the losses squarely. The child does not then go through a natural grieving process that heals the wounds suffered. The tragedies remain a haunting memory for a lifetime. And because he or she fails to face the losses squarely and put them into the past, the child's emotional growth is retarded. In at least one part of the human spirit, the youngster fails to grow up.

As the Task Force members see the situation, compulsive gamblers are emotionally damaged human beings. They grow up emotionally immature, with an unfortunate self-image, low self-esteem, and a poor ability to handle the frustrations, problems, and heartbreaks that life is certain to bring.

As a result, they go in search of pleasure or escape in gambling. In the action and excitement of the play, they seek an escape from the pain of their real or imagined shortcomings. In addition, they seek the confidence and sense of accomplishment that come with winning. Winning and the money it brings also enable them to avoid thinking—at least temporarily—about those frustrations, problems, and heartbreaks with which they are unable to deal because of their emotional immaturity.

If your personality profile suggests that you may be a potential compulsive and if you then decide to try your hand at gambling, you run the risk of becoming trapped in a pattern of behavior familiar to most, if not all, addicted players. They know it as the *deadly pattern*. Unless you are able to break out of it, this pattern invariably leads to disaster. We turn to it now.

THE DEADLY PATTERN

Compulsive gambling shares a trait with other types of addiction. Studies of compulsives show that their gambling usually starts in some small manner that seems quite harmless at that time. Then it follows a definite pattern that eventually leads to disaster. Although in compulsive gambling no substances are taken into the body, the pattern here is similar, and at times identical, to those leading to drug and alcohol addiction.

Pretending again that you are a potential compulsive, let's follow this pattern to see how it develops. Dr. Robert Custer envisions it as being divided into three distinct phases. As usual, we'll talk about the phases as they apply to you, the young player, but we will also point out what happens with adults. Remember, studies show that most adult compulsives started gambling while in their teens.

Your gambling habit can begin in any number of ways—with anything from your first card or bingo game to your first visit to a racetrack. It matters not how you begin. Nor does it matter whether you start because you are interested in gambling or because some friends ask you to join a card game. What counts is that your first experience is a pleasant one; the play—the "action"—proves to be exciting; it relaxes you and takes your mind off your problems. In the words of the drug addict, the experience "gives you a high." And so you want to play again to hit that high once more.[1]

When you continue to play, you may, as many compulsives have done, prefer to stick with the type of gambling that got you started. Or, along with other compulsives, you may want to try several different types of gambling. Whatever the case, you will be careful with your money at this point and will probably devote a good part of your time to learning more about the kind of gambling you prefer and about gambling in general.

Your preference for certain types of gambling may be linked to your sex. Studies made in the 1980s show that males and females have their own preferences. The forms of play most liked by males are, in order of preference, horse racing, sports betting, card games, and dice games. The order of preference for females is card games, slot machines, poker machines (devices that resemble slot machines and allow the player to build hopefully winning poker hands on their screens), horse racing, and lotteries.

(These studies were conducted by Dr. Henry R. Lesieur and Dr. Rena Nora. Dr. Lesieur, as stated earlier, is a professor of sociology at Saint John's University in Jamaica, New York. Dr. Nora serves as chief of psychiatry at the Veterans Administration Hospital at Lyons, New Jersey.)

Regardless of whether you stick with one type of gambling or try several, you soon realize that something is happening to you. You find that you are developing a tolerance for your gambling high. You're becoming used to it. Consequently, in the hope of reaching the same level of excitement or the same sense of escape that you felt before, you're driven to gamble more and to wager somewhat larger sums of money. You're doing what drug addicts do when they develop a tolerance for their drug and increase their dosages.

Though you may lose at times, it is likely that you will win more often than not in your first weeks or months. No one knows why. All that can be said is that the world has long had a name for this phenomenon: beginner's luck.

These wins have led Dr. Robert Custer to describe the opening phase of the pattern as the *winning phase*. (It is also known as the *action* or *escape phase*.) For you, it's an enjoyable and exciting period. But it's also a dangerous one. The wins play upon the personality traits that make you a potential compulsive. They bolster your ego and raise your self-esteem by making you feel that everyone looks up to you because you're a winner. They enable you to forget your problems. They satisfy your love for excitement, risk, and competition. They fill you with a sense of power and importance—and with a sense of optimism that is totally false. You think you're the luckiest person around. You're sure that you can't lose and that you're a skillful gambler.

You feel all these things, no matter whether your wins are for large or small amounts. If you're an adult, they may add up to anything from a few extra dollars to as much as you earn in half a year or more.

If you're a young person, even the smallest wins seem big because you've likely never had much money of your own before. Listen to what a sixty-two-year-old compulsive who swore off gambling twelve years ago has to say about the win that got him started:

Weldon

This all happened back in the 1930s. My family used to go camping every year at a lake. There was a general store there, and it had a penny slot machine in it. One year—I think I must have been around nine or ten—my grandfather gave me about maybe twenty pennies to play in it. I'd just about used them all up when I hit the jackpot—and out came 95 cents. That 95 cents was more money than I'd ever had at one time in my life. I was in heaven. Naturally I had to play some more, and I lost it all and came away with nothing. But that didn't matter. I think I was hooked on gambling from then on. I began pitching pennies with the kids next door and making nickel bets on college football games. Then, in my teens, I graduated to cards.

Large or small, the wins drive you to further play so that you can go on hitting that ego-boosting high. It is not necessary, however, to pass through this winning phase to become a compulsive. There are many players who do not come up with frequent wins at the start of their gambling careers, but still go on to become compulsives. Studies show that more men than women experience the winning phase. This may happen because slot machines are high on the women's list of gambling preferences. Slot-machine play does not require any of the skills that can increase your chances of winning in other games.

One thing can be said for certain about the winning phase: It soon comes to an end. It's impossible to gamble and always win or to consistently win more often than not. Experienced gamblers have a terse explanation for this: If you won all the time, it wouldn't be called gambling.

When you stop winning, you enter the second phase of the deadly pattern. Dr. Custer calls it the *losing phase,* and it really starts you on the long downhill slide to tragedy.

♥ PHASE 2: NOW YOU'RE LOSING

Suddenly luck deserts you. You begin to lose, perhaps steadily, and certainly more often than not.[2] Your losses disturb you deeply. Snatched away with each are the wonderful feelings you had about yourself while winning. Gambling is no longer fun; it is turning into agony. Your ego and self-esteem take a cruel beating, causing you to become depressed, nervous, and unsure of yourself.

You desperately want to experience again all those fine feelings of such a short time ago. And so you go on playing. Now, however, you gamble more often and begin to increase the size of your wagers. Here you're doing more than trying to recapture some vanished feelings. Because you're losing, you're gambling more and risking more in an attempt to win back your losses. For this reason, the losing phase is also known as the *chasing phase,* meaning that you're chasing after your lost money and trying to recover it. You're also starting a way of gambling that will steadily worsen.

About this time you realize, if you stop and think about it, that gambling is becoming an obsession. It's beginning to be on your mind all the time, blotting out all other thoughts. You plan when and where you can make your next bet or play in your next game. You dream up excuses to get out of the house or stay away from school or your job so that you can get to a card or dice game. You begin to lose interest in your friends and in the hobbies and social events that you once enjoyed.

Perhaps most of all you wonder how you can raise the money for your next bet. If you're an adult, you begin using more and more of your salary for gambling and leaving some household bills unpaid. If you're a young person, you ask your parents for extra money for a fictitious purpose; you borrow a little here and there from your friends; you sell some of your personal possessions, perhaps an item of clothing, an old wristwatch, a gift you received last Christmas.

If you bother to take a look at yourself, you'll also see some ugly changes in your personality. In keeping with many potential compulsives, you were once an outwardly cheerful person. Now you're irritable and glum. Your feelings are easily hurt and your temper is frayed, making it easy for you to get into arguments with family and friends. You know that gambling is hurting you and that you should stop before things get worse, but you feel powerless to do so. Your self-esteem is plunging, and you're angry with yourself for your weakness.

Further, you're becoming secretive about your gambling. During your winning phase, you very likely talked, even boasted, to your friends and family about what you were doing. All the talk gave your ego and self-esteem an extra lift. But now you don't want it known that you're losing. You grow angry when someone—friend, parent, relative, teacher—tries to talk to you about what you're doing to yourself.

You may be sure that someone will be worried about your predicament and speak to you about it. It may be someone who knows you are gambling or someone who suspects that your constant need for money is caused by gambling. As an adult, you may be approached by your spouse or employer; your spouse will complain that too many bills are going unpaid; your employer will accuse you of no longer working efficiently and will threaten you with the loss of your job. As a young person, you may be confronted by your parents, your best friend, your favorite teacher; they will argue that you are behaving foolishly, jeopardizing your education, and endangering your chances for a good career later on. Whether you are an adult or a young person, everyone will plead with you to stop gambling.

All these pleas will finally get through to you if you are like most compulsives. You will promise to quit. It's a pledge that you genuinely intend to keep. Everyone will forgive you, and your family may try to help by paying off your debts—perhaps all at once, perhaps in installments.

Time will show that the family is making a mistake here. This is because, try as you might, the chances are overwhelming that you will be unable to keep your promise. The urge to gamble remains. It intensifies as the strains and problems of daily life press in all sides. You live with a sense of defeat that sends your ego and self-esteem plunging still further. If you are trying to repay your family for making good on your losses, money will always be in short supply; this causes you to go more deeply into debt just to meet your monthly bills if you're an adult; it leaves you with little money of your own if you're a young person. After months or even several years of exciting play, you're having trouble concentrating on your job, your education, your responsibilities, and on leading a normal life.

On top of all else, your health is in trouble. Perhaps you're feeling tired and listless all the time. Perhaps you're suffering headaches and stomach upsets. What is happening here is that, along with all the stresses of everyday life, you're coming up against the same problems that drug addicts face when they stop using their drugs—the pains of withdrawal.

Finally, you can no longer stand the stress and the pain. Back to gambling you go—and into the third and final phase of the deadly pattern.

♠ PHASE 3: GAMBLING DESPERATELY

You started your gambling in a small way. But not now, not when you enter the third phase. You plunge in with more play and heavier bets than ever before.[3]

All during the time you were staying away from gambling, you could not be rid of one thought: Though you had been steadily losing when you quit, you remained certain that you could win again, just as you did at the start of things. After all, you had won before. There seemed no reason to think that you could not do so again.

There is, you tell yourself, just a single difference between your situation now and at the time you began gambling. You are now up to your neck in debt. You want to make up your losses quickly or, better yet, on one major all-out bet. For this reason, the third phase is known as the *desperation phase*. What you're doing is frantically running after your lost money in an attempt to regain it. In gambling terms, you're throwing good money after bad.

You were trying, during the losing, or chasing, phase, to win back your money. But now things have worsened. You're out of control. You not only gamble more than before but you also gamble recklessly. You make the riskiest sorts of bets because, should they happen to work out, you'll reap a huge profit that will instantly solve all your problems. A member of Gamblers Anonymous, the worldwide organization for compulsives working to be rid of their habit, recalls his history of wagering on horse races:

Ken

I started out with sensible bets. I studied the records of the horses and picked the best one in each race. But the best usually brought odds like 2 to 1. I'd get back only six dollars—the two bucks I'd bet plus a four-dollar profit. But now I got dumb and started to go for long shots at 20- or 40- or even 50-to-1 odds. On a 50-to-1 horse, I could make over $100 for my two bucks. But they never came in, and you can take my word for it that I was betting a lot more than a couple of dollars on them.

Reckless betting almost always ends for you as it did for Ken: You lose. And so, sinking ever deeper into the quicksand of debt, you need more and more money. But how to get it?

You do what you did in your losing phase. You obtain the needed money from any source you can find—but now you're grasping for rapidly growing sums. Various sources are available to you as an adult. As many compulsives have done, you may dig into your checking or savings accounts at the bank, withdrawing money needed to pay household bills or money that has been set aside for some special purpose—a vacation, your child's future education, or a purchase of a new car. You may take out loans from a bank, a loan company, or the credit union at your place of work. You may obtain cash on your credit card. You may borrow from your employer, obtain advances on your salary, or remove money from your pension fund. You may borrow from friends and relatives. It is almost a certainty that you will try all these methods. Perhaps, as one woman did, you will go even further and be driven to the humiliation of borrowing from your teenage children.

Her name is Helen, and she was one of the fifty women compulsives interviewed in the Henry R. Lesieur study mentioned in Chapter 4. She told him that

> Her seventeen-year-old son was working and earning $178 a week. She first asked for a loan from the boy to help repay $500 that she had obtained on her MasterCard, saying that if his father found out about the debt, he would fly into a rage. But the money did not go toward her credit card debt. It ended up in slot machines. She borrowed still more and, in time, owed her son $3,000.

If you are a young person, you probably follow the same path as the adult. Just as you did in your losing phase, you hit your salary and, if you have them, your checking and savings accounts at the bank. You borrow from anyone you can find—your parents, your brothers and sisters, your relatives, and your friends. You may even go so far as to try to borrow from a bank or a loan company. When your debts become too great, you may turn to a relative to help you pay them off. The Lesieur-Klein study of 892 New Jersey high school students (see Chapter 1) found that almost 7 percent of the young gamblers had borrowed from four or more sources or had sought the assistance of a relative to pay off a heavy debt.

Though you will likely be able to borrow less than the adult, it is possible that the amount will end up being sizable, as was the case with the teenage girl in Chapter 1. Her play in the Atlantic City casinos eventually cost her more than $5,000, some of it her own money, some of it her family's.

No matter whether you're a young person or an adult, the chances are that you honestly plan to pay back all the borrowed money and will make the effort to do so. This holds true for most compulsives. In great part, your efforts are meant to placate your various loan sources so that you can return to them later for more money. Your attempts to keep everyone happy can cause your loans and repayments, especially if you're an adult, to enter what is called a spiral pattern. As explained by a member of Gamblers Anonymous, the spiral works this way:

George

Say you borrow fifty bucks from a friend. You want to keep on his good side, so you really bend over backwards to pay him back. So you go to another friend and hit him up for seventy-five bucks. Now you've got enough to pay back the first guy, plus another twenty-five to play with. Then, if you want to keep the second guy happy, you go to someone else and borrow, say, maybe ninety or a hundred so that you got enough for the second guy and some left over. Then you start over with the first guy and repeat the process. At the same time, you add more people to your list.

Once you're in the spiral, you see that it can be tried with other sources. You begin using it on banks, loan companies, and your credit cards, borrowing from one for a gambling stake and from another to pay back the first and have a little left over for more play.

The spiral may work for a time, but it's bound to end. Betting recklessly and continuing to lose, you eventually need sums too great for your friends to loan. Any number of things can now happen. You may search for other friends to tap, finally ending up with so many creditors that you can't remember them all. You may turn to loan sharks and worsen things by being required to pay an exorbitantly high rate of interest on the amount borrowed. You may begin stalling your creditors, promising to pay them back tomorrow or next week or next payday, whenever they see you. But you do everything possible to keep away from them. You don't answer your telephone. You refuse invitations to parties, family get-togethers, class reunions—to any function where a friend or relative might approach you with an extended hand, palm upturned.

There finally comes that time when you can no longer borrow. You owe so much that you're unable to repay anyone. No one will trust you with another cent.

By now—or even before now—your need for money and your obsession with gambling have blunted your sense of right and wrong. You begin to use illegal means to get the cash for your next bet. As a young person, you may find yourself turning in several directions. You may begin to steal from your parents, taking a few dollars from your mother's purse or your father's wallet. You may begin to dip into the cash register or the petty cash box at work. You may break into a friend's locker at school. As one young man admitted during a gambling study in the late 1970s, he had even tried drug peddling.

Or, in imitation of Ben, the New Jersey teenager whose arrest was reported in Chapter 1, you may begin to burglarize the homes in town for cash or for goods that you can then sell. Before Ben finished, he had stolen items worth $10,000.

In the Lesieur-Klein study of New Jersey students, 10 percent of the young people admitted to engaging in illegal activities to raise gambling money. Five percent said they sold drugs, while 3 percent admitted to shoplifting and 4 percent to stealing in other ways. The percentages given for each type of juvenile offense add up to 12 percent rather than the student total of 10 percent because some of the young people committed two or more of the offenses.

The illegal ways in which you, as an adult, can raise money are various. You may choose to engage in loan fraud—that is, borrow money from a loan company using a false name or the name of a friend. You may forge the names of friends on checks that you've stolen. You may pilfer items from your company for resale. A number of women compulsives, when questioned in gambling studies, have admitted turning to prostitution for the money needed to make their next wager or to help pay their debts.

The list of offenses committed by adult compulsives is far longer than the four examples given above. Studies conducted in the mid-1980s by gambling researchers Lesieur and Klein, Sheila B. Blume, and Richard M. Zoppa revealed that compulsives have committed the following criminal acts to feed their habit or pay their debts:

Loan fraud
Check forgery
Forgery
Tax evasion
Tax fraud
Larceny
Burglary
Armed robbery
Pimping
Prostitution
Drug selling
Fencing stolen goods
Bookmaking or working in illegal games
Running a con game to swindle suckers
Hustling at pool, bowling, or some other sport
Embezzlement

Embezzlement is the theft of funds from your employer. One of the most astonishing examples of embezzlement for gambling came to light in Canada a few years ago. It concerned a young bank executive:

> At age twenty-four, Brian Molony was the assistant manager in a Toronto bank. He was also a compulsive gambler. To raise money for his play, he established a series of fictitious savings accounts at the bank. There was no money in any of the accounts, but Molony created bank records showing that each contained a substantial amount. Then he regularly withdrew money from the accounts and traveled down to Atlantic City. By the time his fraud was discovered, he had embezzled the staggering sum of $10 million—the largest bank swindle in Canadian history. He was arrested, sent to trial for fraud, and sentenced to six years in prison. When his wins and losses over the years at the casinos and at racetracks were totaled, it was found that he had gambled away over $457 million.

As you slide deeper into the desperation phase, you lose more than your sense of right and wrong. Vanishing also is your rationality, your common sense. It may be so far gone that you do not consider your thefts, your embezzlements, and your forgeries to be crimes. In your mind, you are taking loans—loans that you fully intend to pay back when you begin to win again.

If you are like many compulsives, your patience, too, will be vanishing. You no longer borrow or steal to raise money for a bet or a game tomorrow or next Saturday or next week. You borrow to gamble *today* because you need to gamble *today*. If you lose, off you go to raise whatever cash you can in any way you can so that you can get back to the play as soon as possible. Your impatience combines with the loss of your rationality and your sense of right and wrong to produce another problem: You no longer care that you are hurting and alienating all the people around you in your constant quest for money. Your only concern is to get the money—and get it right now.

If you sink low enough, you may join Ralph, a compulsive whom Dr. Robert Custer quotes in *When Luck Runs Out*. Broke and wanting $200 to bet on the horses one day, he went to his mother with the story that he needed the money to make good on a bad check he had written. If he failed to do so, he told her, he would be thrown in jail:

> My mother was eighty years old. She was all bent from having worked at a sewing machine in the factory most of her life. I had already gotten $35,000 from her. That was what she had left from her savings and what she got out of my father's insurance when he died. I had cleaned out all that. And now she was living on her Social Security with a little pension. She started to cry and pleaded with me, "Ralphie, what do you want from me? I gave you everything. Now you want to take the food out of my mouth. No. I can't give it to you."
>
> I didn't even hear what she was saying. I had to have the money. So I got on my knees and began to cry and I promised her by all the saints that this was the last time, that I would just pay off that check and my gambling would be finished. I would go straight and my wife and kids would get all my salary. And she believed me. She went down to the bank with me and cashed her Social Security check and gave me $200. An hour later I was at the track.

Over your head in debt, in trouble with everyone who has made you a loan, guilty of illegal acts, perhaps out of a job, suffering a ruined reputation, and gripped by a habit over which you have no control, you're now reaching the end of the three-phrase descent. You are, in the words of the compulsives who have been there, about to "hit rock bottom" or "bottom out."

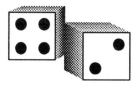

HITTING ROCK BOTTOM

It was a living hell. No. It was a whole collection of living hells.

This is the way one recovering compulsive describes his life in the days just before he bottomed out. He goes on:

> My health was ruined. My mind was in a mess. I had no way of paying my debts. I was in trouble with my family and looking at a divorce. I didn't know which way to turn. I even thought about killing myself.

In just a few terse sentences, he illustrates all that researchers, among them Dr. Robert Custer, have learned of life near and at rock bottom in their work with and studies of compulsive gamblers. Dr. Custer is the psychiatrist who, along with other experts, sees the downhill slide to compulsive gambling as being divided into three phases. He says that during the last days or weeks of the desperation phase, and then the arrival at rock bottom, the compulsive's life can be marked by an assortment of problems. Topping the list are the following five:

> Feelings of hopelessness
> Withdrawal symptoms when, with all gambling money gone, the player is forced to, or decides to, quit.
> The danger of an emotional breakdown.
> Heavy drinking that can—and often does—lead to alcoholism. (Drug addiction is also a danger.)
> Thoughts of or attempts at suicide.[1]

Let's now see the harm these five problems can cause you as a young or an adult compulsive. In the next chapter we'll look at what they can do to your family. We'll also talk of another problem mentioned by Dr. Custer—the upheavals that can see the compulsive's relations with his or her family members destroyed for years—or for all time.

We begin with your health.

◆ **YOUR HEALTH**

It goes without saying that all your experiences along the way to rock bottom, plus your feelings on landing there, are bound to damage severely both your physical and emotional health.[2] Also, the fact that you've been playing at all hours and spending the rest of your time frantically searching for money is going to exact a toll on your health, especially your body's resistance to illness.

The kinds of physical and emotional damage are many. They are described in a study made during the 1980s by Dr. Valerie C. Lorenz and Dr. Robert A. Yaffee. (Dr. Lorenz is the executive director of the National Center for Pathological Gambling. Dr. Yaffee is a research consultant with the Academic Computing Facility of New York University's Courant Institute of Mathematical Sciences.)

The two researchers prepared a questionnaire on the health problems suffered by compulsives during the desperation phase. In 1983 and 1984 it was answered by 206 members of Gamblers Anonymous (GA), who ranged in age from fifteen to seventy-seven. In their responses they spoke of complaints extending from feelings of deep depression to incidents of temporary amnesia. Below is a representative list of the complaints and the number of GA members who suffered them. (The number of gamblers reporting the complaints far exceeds the total of 206 members who participated in the survey. Some members reported suffering a combination of disorders.)

NO. OF MEMBERS	COMPLAINT
94 (46%)	Depression
86 (42%)	Abdominal problems such as loose bowels, knotted stomach, excessive gas, constipation, colitis
73 (35%)	Insomnia
63 (31%)	Faintness or dizziness; clammy or sweaty hands; heavy perspiration
60 (29%)	Headaches, including migraines
36 (18%)	Asthma
35 (17%)	High blood pressure
35 (17%)	Backache
33 (16%)	Angina, heart pain, heart palpitation
29 (14%)	Stiff neck
25 (12%)	Excessive urination
24 (12%)	Dermatitis, hives, rash
18 (9%)	Ulcers
9 (4%)	Temporary amnesia

The National Council on Problem Gambling reports that many compulsives also suffer serious psychiatric illnesses. For example, the council points to a 1980s study made of fifty compulsives at the time they were patients in Veterans Administration hospitals. The study found that 76 percent of the compulsives were suffering major depressions. Thirty-six percent were afflicted with hypomania, a mild form of mania (the term *mania* refers to the excitement and disorganized behavior associated with insanity). Six percent were burdened with a more severe mania.

With your physical and mental health in shambles, you risk an emotional breakdown. Withdrawal symptoms—the intense nervousness, the awful shortness of temper, and the physical pain that plague you when you attempt or are forced to quit gambling—may also lead to a breakdown. An emotional breakdown is usually incapacitating, making it impossible for you to perform the simplest of everyday tasks. It often requires hospitalization and a long period of recuperation. It is possible, however, that the hospitalization and then the period of recuperation, taking you away from gambling as they do, will mark the first steps along the way to ridding yourself of your compulsion.

Many compulsives are so troubled by their physical and emotional ills and the possibility of a breakdown that they seek professional help. Three studies made in the 1970s and 1980s demonstrate this pattern. The first two studies looked at more than 150 male members of Gamblers Anonymous and found that 20 to 40 percent of their number had turned to health professionals for assistance prior to joining GA. The third study surveyed fifty women members of Gamblers Anonymous and discovered that 58 percent had sought help before joining the organization.

The study of the fifty women was conducted by Dr. Henry R. Lesieur. Thirteen of the women told him that they had suffered hallucinations. One hallucinated at the close of several days of continual gambling in Nevada casinos, prompting Dr. Lesieur to think that the experience was triggered by lack of sleep.

The women were also asked if they believed they had shown symptoms of paranoia. (Paranoia is a disorder in which the victim develops delusions of grandeur or persecution.) Thirteen women admitted to paranoid symptoms that were more than transitory. Two admitted to a deep fear of loan sharks, with Dr. Lesieur believing they had legitimate reason to be frightened. Three appeared to harbor an irrational fear that people were following them.

The Lesieur study found that all but three of the hallucinatory experiences were connected with drug use. The study also found that five of the instances of paranoid behavior seemed to be related to the use of amphetamines. These findings bring us to the next of the health dangers facing the compulsive.

♣ DUAL ADDICTION

It is quite likely that, as a compulsive, you will develop what is called *dual addiction*.[3] This means that you will develop one or more other addictions in addition to your gambling compulsion.

Studies conducted in the 1980s show the most common addiction suffered by compulsives is substance abuse, with the most commonly abused substance being alcohol.

For example, Dr. Joseph Ciarrocchi, the director of addiction services at Taylor Manor Hospital in Maryland, reports that his 1985 study of compulsives with dual addiction revealed that 92 percent of their number abused alcohol. Smaller but still significant percentages admitted to abusing marijuana (33 percent), amphetamines (25 percent), cocaine (17 percent), barbiturates (8 percent), and hallucinogens (also 8 percent). The study involved twelve patients at the hospital.

Another finding: A study of members of Gamblers Anonymous found that 52 percent of their number had problems with alcohol or drug abuse or both.

Still another finding: When the patients in a program for compulsives at Veterans Administration hospitals were surveyed, 47 percent admitted to having abused alcohol or drugs at some point in their lives.

Finally: A study of alcoholics at the South Oaks Hospital in Amityville, New York, revealed that 20 percent of their number had a problem with gambling. About half the problem gamblers were compulsives.

As if your medical problems aren't bad enough on hitting rock bottom, they are even worse if you are the victim of dual addiction. Dr. Ciarrocchi, when writing of his study in a 1987 issue of the *Journal of Gambling Behavior*, pointed out that his twelve patients suffered not only the asthma, hives, heart conditions, and ulcers endured by other compulsives but also seizures, gum disease, loose teeth, and emphysema.

Further, he stated that the medical problems of 66 percent of the patients under study were chronic conditions. He added that 100 percent of the patients were seriously depressed and then remarked that compulsive gamblers who are substance abusers are more prone to psychiatric problems than those who are not.

Alcoholism and drug abuse are crutches that can

be easily picked up and leaned on as you hobble off into forgetfulness, trying to escape your problems. Alcohol has always loomed as a great menace because it has traditionally been available wherever there is gambling. It is a particular hazard in today's casinos, where free drinks are routinely offered to the players. On the surface, they are proffered as a courtesy to the customers. Below the surface, the aim is to loosen up the players and encourage them to continue gambling with increasing abandon.

Alcoholism and drug addiction are not the only problems that go hand in hand with compulsive gambling. Some of the women whom Dr. Lesieur interviewed also admitted such addictions as overeating and overspending. Twelve told him that they had gone on spending sprees that had cost them thousands of dollars. He noted that these spending sprees seemed to occur most frequently when the women were attempting to stop gambling.

As a compulsive, regardless of your age, it is likely that you'll be saddled with a problem that is common among alcoholics and addicted drug users— denial. It is the denial, to yourself and all others, that you are actually a compulsive and that your gambling habit is behind the disaster you have made of your life. There can be a number of reasons for your denial. For one, you may have fooled yourself into honestly believing that you're all right.

Even when, down deep inside, you do recognize your compulsion, you may still refuse to admit it to yourself and to all the people in your life. Here, you may be too embarrassed to face up to the problem. Or you may be afraid to see yourself as weak, helpless, and destructive. Or you may fear that, once you admit your compulsion, you will have to endure the discomfort of ending your gambling and beginning the struggle back to a normal life.

There are steps you can take to help yourself overcome the problem of denial and start along that road back to a normal life. We're going to talk about them in the closing chapters of this book.

♥ SUICIDE

One of the most tragic problems affecting tortured compulsives is the risk of suicide.[4] The idea of doing away with themselves invades their minds when their debilitated physical and emotional condition seems too painful to bear. Dr. Custer remarks that one in five compulsives attempts to commit suicide. Dr. Lesieur, in *The Chase: Career of the Compulsive Gambler*, writes of the years he spent interviewing compulsives and of what he learned of the part suicide played in their lives: "There are stories at GA meetings of friends who have shot themselves, died in auto accidents, or killed themselves by carbon monoxide poisoning. . . . Half the compulsive gamblers I interviewed seriously contemplated suicide." The players told him of the various methods they had considered for doing away with themselves. The methods ranged from death by gunshot to death in a deliberate automobile crash. The latter was preferred by 50 percent of the compulsives. Dr. Lesieur explains the reasons why: "Death in an automobile is thought to be relatively fast (especially driving off a cliff) and had the added incentive of being insurable."

What the gamblers were thinking of here is a basic provision in life insurance policies: The insurance will be paid if the insured person dies in an accident but not if he or she commits suicide. One gambler told Dr. Lesieur of how this provision was on his mind during some awful moments:

> I had a tank of gas one night, riding around one night trying to get enough nerve; I drove around the reservoir. And I even thought about committing suicide with the car . . . [but] if I did it my wife wouldn't get any insurance money. I figured, jees, if I'm gonna commit suicide I want to fix it so it looked like an accident. . . . After all the misery I caused I could at least leave her with the bills paid, anyway.

Dr. Lesieur goes on to write that he found the contemplation of suicide to be far more common among married gamblers than among unmarried ones. This may be because the actions of the unmarried gambler—whether a young person or an adult—do not usually destroy a family's finances. Unmarried adults, though drowning in bills, are chiefly responsible just to themselves and do not drag a spouse and children down into the pits of debt with them. Unmarried young people, while they may have borrowed or stolen from their parents, are usually unable to break into and empty the family checkbook.

It may also be that most young people, even if greatly disturbed, have a greater desire to live than do older persons. And young people may not be as sensitive to and distressed by the harm they are doing.

Some gamblers, Dr. Lesieur continues, have taken out life insurance policies and then, while not actually attempting suicide, have hoped that they would somehow be killed in an accident. They have "hoped they would get a blowout in their car or prayed their plane would crash. In a sense they deliberately gambled with death, hoping it would come about without overt action on their part."

There were deterrents that kept some who were seriously considering suicide from acting. Some could not raise the money for a life insurance policy or were turned down for health or other reasons.

Some bought life insurance and then realized that it would not cover their debts and leave enough for their families to start life anew. Some could not bring themselves to commit suicide because of their moral beliefs. Some turned away because of the sorrow it would bring to their loved ones. One such compulsive is a woman named Kathy, whom Dr. Lesieur quotes in his booklet *Understanding Compulsive Gambling*: "I was suicidal. . . . I had a gun to my head, and I think the only thing that stopped me was the thought of my daughter finding my brains all over the wall. I just couldn't do that to her." Kathy also worried about the harm that might be done to strangers: "I thought several times last year about running my car off the road. I thought about running it into another automobile but I thought I would kill somebody else."

Regardless of your age, you may suffer any one or any combination of the problems we've discussed, as well as others. They are terrible. And they are made worse by the fact that you are not enduring them alone as you slide through the desperation phase and at last hit rock bottom. Descending with you—and suffering as much as you in their own way—are the members of your family. We turn to them now for a close look at their anguish and a further look at your own.

YOUR FAMILY: AT ROCK BOTTOM WITH YOU

To see what your compulsion does to your family members, we're going to look at each of them in turn, beginning with your parents if you are an unmarried young person. Then, pretending that you're married, we'll look at your spouse and your children. All that we will have to say is based on studies made of the families of compulsives.

♠ YOUR PARENTS

Your parents can be expected to react in several ways to your gambling problem. They'll usually begin by denying to themselves and everyone else that you have a problem.[1] Their denial will cause them to do three things. They'll make excuses for your behavior, lie for you when people ask if you're in some sort of trouble, and give or lend you money to repay your debts—and sometimes even for further play.

Their financial help, of course, puts a terrible strain on the family budget. In their efforts to help, the parents commonly do just what the compulsives themselves do—dig into a savings account and drop their plans for a vacation or the purchase of a new car. And some families, when an exorbitant amount is owed, have gone so far as to mortgage their homes to raise the needed cash.

Both your mother and your father will at first react to your gambling in much the same manner. But if they behave like the parents of most compulsives, they will soon begin to react in individual ways. Your father, for example, will probably rebel against the whole situation. He may well turn his back on you and refuse to provide you with further money. He may criticize your poor performance in school or on the job. You'll likely hear that you are weak and irresponsible and haven't the guts to overcome your growing compulsion.

Your mother, however, may well become protective. She may, for example, continue to deny your problem for a time longer. Or she may go on making excuses for your behavior and lying about your gambling to anyone who asks. And it is probable that she will go on giving you money to pay your debts or to make your next bet. In most cases, she'll quietly slip the money to you without your father's knowledge.

Their differing reactions to your problem are almost sure to cause trouble between your parents, perhaps causing the following to happen: Your father, already down on you, grows angry with his wife because of her protective attitude. His anger explodes into fury when he learns that she has been secretly giving you money. For her part, your mother becomes angry with your father for turning his back on you.

Along with their anger, your parents may experience a number of other emotions. For instance, your mother, on finally admitting your problem, will be hit with feelings that swing back and forth between two extremes. One minute she'll love you, and the next she'll hate you for what you're doing to the family. One minute she'll feel a deep guilt for having raised a "sick" or "weak" child, and the next, because she's unable to endure her sense of guilt, she'll tell herself that she's not at fault for your habit and that you're responsible for your own behavior and should know better.

Along with your father's anger there may be a deep sense of humiliation; he'll tell himself that your habit is a weakness that is causing everyone to think that his family is made up of weaklings. He may also feel that your mother has betrayed him by slipping you money behind his back.

These feelings can strain your parents' marriage to the breaking point. If the marriage is not a strong one in the first place, they can easily lead to divorce, and have done so in many cases.

Regardless of their individual feelings, your parents will likely come to your aid when you finally decide that you must end your gambling. With both desperately wanting you to be your old self again, they will probably pay or help to pay for treatment by a psychiatrist or psychologist or at a hospital with a recovery program for compulsives. Should you join Gamblers Anonymous, they will undoubtedly encourage you to attend the meetings and will assist in sustaining your determination to defeat your compulsion.

Your mother and father may also try to help by learning more about your problem. They may join Gam-Anon, an organization that is affiliated with Gamblers Anonymous and is meant for the families of compulsives. There they can take advantage of what its members have to say and advise while at the same time helping the other members by speaking of their own experiences. Or they may seek private psychiatric or psychological help. In most cases they will need to learn not only how to assist you but also how to survive with a gambling problem in the family and how to repair the damage it has done to their marriage.

◆ YOUR SPOUSE

Now let's move ahead to your adulthood and say that you are married. As your parents did when you were young, your wife or your husband will react to your problem in individual ways.[2] If you happen to be the child of a compulsive, please read the following with an eye to understanding what your non-gambling parent is going through and how he or she is reacting to the whole problem.

♣ Your Wife

Your wife faces the same problems as you during your descent to rock bottom. She, too, endures feelings of hopelessness. She, too, is threatened by the possibility of a mental breakdown. She, too, harbors terrible thoughts of suicide.

As a result, her physical and emotional health is harmed. Dr. Valerie C. Lorenz and Dr. Robert A. Yaffee submitted their health questionnaire not only to members of Gamblers Anonymous in 1983 and 1984 (see Chapter 6) but also to the wives of some of the members themselves. It was answered by 206 women. Their answers matched many of those given by their husbands. Among their health complaints, which they experienced singly or in some combination, were the following:

NO. OF WOMEN	COMPLAINT
101 (47%)	Depression
89 (41%)	Chronic or severe headaches
79 (37%)	Irritable bowels, constipation, diarrhea
57 (27%)	Faintness, dizziness, cold and clammy hands, excessive perspiration
30 (14%)	Asthma
23 (11%)	High blood pressure

Thirty of the wives admitted to harboring thoughts of suicide. One hundred fifty-eight said they felt angry with or resentful of their husbands. Ninety-five reported feeling isolated from the spouse and feeling lonely or alone. Sixty-five said they felt guilty and responsible for causing or contributing to the husband's gambling.

Your wife's feelings of isolation, anger, and guilt take shape as she watches you slide through the deadly pattern to rock bottom. Research shows that many wives pass through a three-phase pattern of their own. The phases are:

♥ **THE DENIAL PHASE** This period occurs at the start of your gambling. Sensing or knowing of the gambling, your wife begins to worry about what the future holds. But she keeps her concerns to herself at this time and does not speak up when your gambling increases, preferring instead to look on it as something temporary. She does, however, question you about the growing number of unpaid bills, but feels reassured when you insist that all is well and that the bills will soon be paid.

Throughout this opening phase, she behaves much as your parents do. She denies to herself and others that you have a problem. She makes excuses for your behavior and lies about your gambling to friends and relatives. She is also forgiving when you show remorse for what you are doing.

♠ **THE STRESS PHASE** This period coincides with your losing (chasing) phase and the increased gambling and changes in your personality that it triggers. It is a time of growing stress for the wife—a time of arguments over the bills due, over your lost time at work, and over your declining interest in the family as your obsession with gambling flowers. It is also the time when the wife attempts to control money matters by taking over the family checkbook, and the time when she begins to feel a deep resentment of your gambling and demands that you put a stop to it.

Nevertheless, if she is like the wives of many compulsives, she quickly provides the money needed to bail you out when your gambling debts threaten to swamp you. Also, to avoid a family fight, she usually gives in to your pleas for enough money to make your next bet. The National Council on Problem Gambling reports that over half the wives of compulsives have borrowed from friends and family to come up with the cash for further gambling. Well over half have dipped into their personal savings to do so, and close to half have handed over some of their earnings.

♦ **THE EXHAUSTION PHASE** As you plunge into the desperation phase, your wife admits to herself the terrible truth of your compulsion. This fills her with anxiety—even panic—as does your total immersion in gambling, your poor performance at work (you may even have lost your job by now), your worsening reputation among family and friends, and the ever-mounting number of unpaid loans and household bills. The family debts are now at flood tide, and she turns wherever she can to raise the money to keep the family from drowning in them.

According to the National Council on Problem Gambling, a majority of the wives of compulsives have borrowed from friends and relatives to meet the basic needs of the family. A majority have also been harassed or even threatened by creditors. Employers have threatened to garnishee the gambler's wages (meaning they would withhold a portion of his earnings) to make good on loans or salary advances. Merchants have promised to repossess family cars and furniture. Banks and loan companies have threatened to foreclose on home mortgages. Other creditors have threatened to sue for the money due them or to have the gambler arrested for some illegal act, such as theft or embezzlement.

By now your wife is exhausted by all that is happening. The resentment she has long felt for your gambling turns to rage. She is furious at the harm you're inflicting on everyone. She is humiliated by all the borrowing—yours to finance your next bet, hers to keep the family afloat. Her exhaustion leads to confusion. She doesn't know how to stop your gambling, where to get help for you, or how to pay the mountain of bills once there is no one left to make her a loan. Her confusion impairs her thinking and leaves her feeling immobilized—unable to find any solution to the tragic problem. She becomes prey to the physical and emotional disorders that the Lorenz-Yaffee questionnaire brought to light.

♣ **AT ROCK BOTTOM** At last she hits her own rock bottom. There, she not only shares your sense of hopelessness but also feels a sense of helplessness because she has been unable to put an end to your gambling and find a way to save her family from disaster. Along with you, she faces the threat of a mental breakdown and may consider—or even attempt—suicide. The National Council on Problem Gambling reports that 11 percent of the wives of compulsives have tried to end their lives. One study shows that they are four times more likely to commit suicide than are people in the general population.

One of your major fears at rock bottom is the possibility that your wife will leave you and perhaps seek a divorce. This is a more than reasonable fear. A study made in the late 1970s revealed that the incidence of separation and divorce is far higher among compulsives than among the general population. Compulsive gamblers are more likely than the average person to have been married two or three times.

♥ Your Husband

While wives are patient with their gambling husbands for a long while, studies show that the same cannot usually be said of the husbands of gambling wives. If your husband is like most others, he will be impatient with your gambling from the moment he learns of it. Much of his impatience will stem from the fact that your growing compulsion has drastically changed you and the way life is lived in your home.

Before being caught up in a frenzy of play, you assumed many responsibilities—caring for your home and family, your job, and your personal commitments. But now your mind is on your next bet. Clothes are unwashed. Meals are not prepared on time or, on occasion, at all. Your employer or associates complain about your performance. You no longer seem interested in your work or your husband's or in your children's education. On top of all else, you are gone much of the time, often staying out most or all of the night to gamble. Your husband and children feel ignored and even abandoned.

Impatient though he may be, your husband will probably give you the money to pay off your first debts. But he is less likely than the wife of a compulsive to go on bailing you out for an extended period. And he is less likely than the wife to be patient with your problem for a long period. Rather, he is more apt to insist in a short while that you take hold of yourself and be rid of your growing compulsion.

Should you receive any encouragement to seek treatment for your gambling, it will likely come not from your husband but from your children, especially if they are grown, from a relative, or from a close friend. Then, when you do seek treatment, your husband will often prove less willing than the compulsive's wife to learn more about the gambling habit so that he can assist in overcoming it. For example, should you turn to Gamblers Anonymous, he will usually shy away from joining Gam-Anon and hearing what its members have to say to the spouses of compulsives.

While separation or divorce is always a threat to the male compulsive, it is a particular threat to the woman. The husband is customarily far more reluctant to stay with a marriage than is the wife of a compulsive.

♠ YOUR CHILDREN

Again, we move forward to your adulthood—now to the time when you are a parent. And if you are the child of a compulsive, you may wish to read the coming paragraphs much as you did the material on the wife and husband. You will then be able to compare your experiences with those of other children in homes with a gambling problem. In all likelihood, you'll see that you are not alone in your experiences and feelings.

In *When Luck Runs Out: Help for Compulsive Gamblers and Their Families*, Dr. Robert Custer writes that your children may at first be happy with your gambling.[3] This is because you may shower them with gifts during your winning phase and take them to places that other parents are unable to afford. There will be no doubt in the children's minds that you love them very much.

But this happy period ends with the arrival of your losing (chasing) phase. Becoming more and more preoccupied with gambling, you begin to ignore and neglect your children. No longer do you march into the house with surprise gifts. No longer are there visits to amusement parks. Ignored and neglected, the children feel the first pangs of a pain that will intensify as time passes.

The hurt intensifies when you go far beyond ignoring and neglecting the youngsters. Frustrated by your losses, you start to take out that frustration on them. You angrily push them away when they seek your help or companionship at a time when you can think only of your next bet. You scold them—and often punish them too harshly—for some minor misbehavior or mistake. You may even fly into a rage at times and lash out at them physically.

If the children are very young (and this applies to many older ones as well), they may blame themselves for your actions and think that they have done something bad. Dr. Custer explains that they are not yet mature enough to realize that it is some demon in you that is driving you to act as you do and not something that they are doing.

The children at first lock their hurt and their mistaken feelings of guilt inside themselves. At this point the non-gambling parent, especially the mother, may comfort them and try to ease their pain. But then, as she becomes sickened by what the gambling is doing to the family, she is less and less able to give them the love and attention they so desperately need. The children feel more lost and rejected than ever before and, in time, become the victims of a wide variety of physical and emotional upsets and ills.

Dr. Custer writes of what commonly happens to many smaller children: "They cry and whine. They begin to have eating and sleeping problems. They wake up with nightmares and night terrors or walk in their sleep. They refuse to sleep by themselves any longer or with the lights out. . . . They become either rambunctious or cantankerous or silent and withdrawn. Their physical resistance wears down, and they come down with colds, the flu, and other illnesses. They develop phobias, anxieties, enuresis (involuntary wetting, usually bed wetting), facial twitches. If they are already in school, they get sick in school and have to be sent home, or they get sick in the morning and so cannot go to school. In school, they become inattentive, lethargic, troublesome."

And what of older children? Dr. Custer writes that they may share some of the problems experienced by the younger ones. In addition, they may vent their feelings in such misbehaviors as playing truant, running away from home, using alcohol and drugs, engaging in sexual activities, and trying their hand at theft and other antisocial acts. They may become depressed and develop a variety of physical and emotional disorders, among them asthma, headaches, and intestinal upsets.

Two studies conducted in the late 1980s point

up the problems borne by the children of compulsive gamblers. The first was led by Dr. Durand F. Jacobs, whose research into teenage gambling was described in Chapter 1. With five colleagues, he surveyed 844 students in four Southern California high schools. Of their number, 52 reported being of families where one or both parents suffered a gambling problem. The remaining 792 said there was no gambling problem at home. The study listed them as having "average parents."

The study found a heavier use of tobacco, alcohol, and drugs among the students with problem-gambling parents than among those with average parents. They also did more overeating. They admitted to starting the use of cigarettes and various drugs at an earlier age than did the other students. The children of average parents, however, began to drink alcohol at a slightly earlier age.

There was also trouble in the following areas for the youngsters with problem gamblers as parents:

> Thirty-seven percent suffered a broken home through separation, divorce, or the death of a parent before reaching age fifteen. This figure was almost twice as high as that for the children with average parents—20 percent.

> Thirty-eight percent said they felt insecure in their lives—as opposed to 20 percent of their fellow students.

> Twenty-five percent admitted feeling emotionally "down" and "unhappy with life and myself"—more than twice the 11 percent reported by the students with average parents.

Further evidence of the emotional problems faced by the children of compulsives comes from the second study, conducted by Dr. Henry R. Lesieur and Jerome Rothschild. On questioning 105 teenage children of Gamblers Anonymous members they learned that 70 percent of the youngsters felt angry most of the time about the parent's gambling, 60 percent felt hurt, and 56 percent depressed while 45 percent felt hateful, 31 percent abandoned, and 26 percent guilty.

In a report of their study, researchers Lesieur and Rothschild write that compulsive gamblers are twice as likely to be physically abusive of their children as are parents in the general population. Gamblers with other problems, such as alcohol abuse, are three times more likely than other parents to abuse their children.

One finding in the Jacobs study indicated that the youngsters of compulsives may end up being compulsives themselves. Seventy-five percent of the students from problem-gambling families said they were already gambling, and had started doing so before age eleven. Only 34 percent of the children in the non-problem families said they had begun to gamble.

There is an organization that is dedicated to assisting the children of compulsives—Gam-A-Teen. Like Gam-Anon, it is affiliated with Gamblers Anonymous and helps teenagers to meet the personal and family problems caused by their gambling parent or parents and to build happy and productive lives for themselves.

More information on both Gam-Anon and Gam-A-Teen—including how to contact them for assistance—is contained in the next chapter.

There comes a time at rock bottom when, torn by your own feelings and those of your loved ones, you resolve to end your gambling and start back along the path to a normal life. It is a difficult uphill path that you face. But it is one that you need not travel alone. There are helping hands waiting for you along the way.

THE ROAD BACK

Once you quit gambling—and stick to your resolve never to wager again—you will find that the road back to a normal life follows a pattern that is the exact opposite of the pattern that sent you plunging to rock bottom. Studies show that it resembles the deadly pattern in only one way: it is divided into three phases. But they are phases marked by a growing number of positive attitudes and actions rather than the negative ones that accompanied you on your downhill slide.

♦ THE THREE-PHASE PATTERN TO RECOVERY

Each of the three phases that make up the pattern has a name: *critical*, *rebuilding*, and *growth*.[1]

♣ The Critical Phase
This opening phase comes by its name for a simple reason. The time immediately following the decision to break *any* long-standing habit is always a

difficult and dangerous one—in a word, a critical one. The temptation to resume the habit is always great. It is especially great for someone who is trying to break a habit as overpowering as compulsive gambling. And so, in this first phase, you'll need to take a very realistic look at yourself and what you've done, and then hold on to that view stubbornly, so that you can remain firm in your determination to find a normal life again.

Then, if you are like the typical recovering compulsive, you will find yourself doing the following as time goes by. You will:

♥ Take stock of yourself. You'll look honestly at your strengths and weaknesses so that you can employ the former for your benefit and seek to control and overcome the latter.

♠ Begin to think more clearly and make decisions on how to conduct your life now and in the future.

♦ Examine your spiritual needs (especially if you are of a religious nature) so that you can take steps to help yourself by fulfilling them.

♣ Work to solve the personal, family, social, and job problems that your gambling caused. As a teenager, you'll also set about solving your educational problems.

During the critical period, you will very likely recognize that your gambling habit is going to be so hard to break that you will need help to escape its hold on you. And remembering how powerless you were in its grip, you will also very likely feel a deep and honest desire for that help. We'll talk in a while about the help that is available to you.

♥ **The Rebuilding Phase**
As its name indicates, this phase is marked by attitudes and actions that illustrate that you are now

actually beginning to build a new life for yourself
and the people around you. For example:

- ♠ There will be improved relations with your family—especially your parents if you are young, unmarried, and living
  at home, or with your wife and children if you are married.
- ♦ Your family and friends will begin to trust you again.
- ♣ You will begin to develop goals for the future—the kind of
  person you want to be, where you want to go in life, and
  how you plan to make good on the debts you incurred during
  your downhill slide.

You'll also see some changes taking place in yourself—changes that are the reverse of those you experienced back in your losing phase. You'll be more
relaxed than you've been in a long while. You'll be
more patient in your dealings with others. Your behavior will be less irritating than in the past. Perhaps best of all, as you successfully ward off the
urge to gamble that is sure to crop up time and again,
you'll feel your self-respect returning.

♥ The Growth Phase
Here you are growing because you are now thinking
less of yourself. Rather, you'll find yourself giving
affection to others, making sacrifices for them, and
understanding their needs.

Another indication of your growth will be an increasing willingness to face life's problems as they
come along, plus an increasing willingness to act on
them.

All during your advance through the first two
phases, you'll be plagued by thoughts of gambling.
The urge to bet again will be great. But the third
phase will see your preoccupation with gambling

begin to fade and make you all the more ready for the new life that awaits you at its close.

♠ HELPING HANDS

Until the urge to gamble begins to decrease, it can seem almost overwhelming. The key to recovery is your determination never to place a bet again. Gamblers Anonymous warns that you must not give in to even the smallest of bets, or to bets that seem harmless because they are made in a social setting among friends or family. They can easily lead to more betting and the rebirth of your compulsion. You'll either have to pick yourself up again immediately or start back through the pattern from its beginning. You are in the same bind as the recovering alcoholic who dares not take a single drink because it almost invariably leads to a binge.[2]

Knowing how overpowering your gambling habit is, you may, as said earlier, quickly recognize that you face a seemingly impossible task to re-create a normal life. Fortunately, the assistance you need can be found in several directions.

♦ Personal Professional Care

While their care can be expensive, you can seek individual treatment with a psychiatrist or psychologist. Since you've run up so many debts while gambling, you will probably have to depend on your family to pay for most, if not all, of the therapy. You will undoubtedly have to do so if you are a teenager.

The National Council on Problem Gambling maintains a list of therapists who specialize in the treatment of recovering compulsive gamblers. You or your family can contact the council's office for the names of therapists in your area. The council states that its list is solely for information; the council does not endorse any particular therapist or program of treatment.[3]

The council's main office is located at 445 West 59th Street, New York, New York 10019. The telephone number is (212) 765-3833. The council also operates a telephone hot line: (800) 522-4700.

♣ **Hospital and Health Center Treatment Programs**
There are a number of hospitals across the country that maintain recovery programs for compulsive gamblers.[4] Some require that you remain in the hospital or center while in treatment. Others will accept you on an outpatient basis.

The programs offered by the various hospitals and centers often vary in their details, and so it is difficult to give a general picture of what they offer. Usually, however, the treatment includes individual therapy, group therapy, and training in stress management. Also, therapy is usually provided for the patient's family. Some facilities work with the compulsive gambler as though he or she were an alcoholic, since the two addictions are believed to resemble each other in many ways.

The following is a list of several well-known hospitals and centers:

CPC Westwood Hospital
2112 South Barrington Avenue
Los Angeles, California 90025
(213) 479-4281

Charter Hospital
7000 West Spring Mountain Road
Las Vegas, Nevada 89117
(702) 876-4357 Ext. 170

Connecticut Compulsive Gambling Treatment Program
Greater Bridgeport Community Health Center
1635 Central Avenue
Bridgeport, Connecticut 06606
(203) 579-6934

Taylor Manor Hospital
Gambling Treatment Program
College Avenue
Ellicott City, Maryland 21043
(301) 465-3322

Compulsive Gambling Treatment Center
J. F. Kennedy Medical Center
Edison, New Jersey 08818
(201) 321-7189

Allen Memorial Hospital
Waterloo, Iowa
(319) 390-3193

VA Medical Center
Bay Pines, Florida 33504
(813) 398-6661 (Ext. 4302)

Rocky Mountain Treatment Center
920 Fourth Avenue, North
Great Falls, Montana 59401
(406) 727-8832

Valley Forge Medical Center and Hospital
Addiction Program
1033 West Germantown Pike
Norristown, Pennsylvania 19403
(215) 539-8500

South Oaks Hospital
Gambling Treatment Program
400 Sunrise Highway
Amityville, New York 11701
(516) 264-4000 Ext. 248

The list is far from complete. You can obtain the names of other hospitals and health centers from the National Council on Problem Gambling.

If you are old enough to have served in the military, or after you've served at some future time, you may want to apply to one of the compulsive gambling treatment programs available at a number of Veterans Administration hospitals. You can obtain from the National Council a list of the VA hospitals providing this care, which is publicly funded.

♥ GAMBLERS ANONYMOUS

If you feel that you are unable to afford—or are reluctant to try—private, hospital, or health center treatment, there is an international organization to which you can turn: Gamblers Anonymous (GA).[5] GA has a track record of more than thirty years of successfully helping recovering compulsives—at no required cost to its members.

Gamblers Anonymous describes itself as "a fellowship of men and women who share their experience, strength and hope with each other that they may solve their common problem and help others recover from a gambling problem."

As a young person who wishes to end a gambling habit, you should not shy away from GA because it says it is a "fellowship of men and women." It is also open to teenagers. The only requirement for membership is the desire to be done with gambling.

GA traces its history back to January 1957, when two compulsive gamblers met by chance and began talking of how they were trying to end their addiction. Finding their conversation beneficial, they agreed to meet regularly to help each other. They soon found that their regular meetings were helping them in their resolve not to stumble and begin gambling again.

As they talked on through the weeks, the two men came to agree that, if they were to be free of gambling, they had to bring about a number of character changes in themselves. To assist them in making these changes, they embraced a set of spiritual principles that had been developed by an organization for people trying to overcome a drinking problem, Alcoholics Anonymous (AA).

Out of the talks grew the idea for an organization based on AA and its principles. It was given a similar name, Gamblers Anonymous. It was—and still is—based on the idea that the compulsive is too often helpless to fight his or her addiction alone, but can wage a good fight when joined and supported by other compulsives who also yearn to quit gambling. Conversely, while recovering, the compulsive can support and help his or her fellow gamblers.

Gamblers Anonymous held its first meeting on September 13, 1957, in Los Angeles barely nine months after the two men had met for the first time. Since then, GA has grown steadily, both in the United States and elsewhere. It now has just over 1,100 chapters worldwide, with around 750 of their number located here in the United States. Elsewhere, chapters are to be found in such widely separated countries as Australia, Canada, Great Britain, India, and Korea.

GA takes the word "anonymous" seriously. When

you join, your name is kept private. Other members are urged not to mention it to outsiders, and you are urged not to mention theirs. You are free, however, to tell anyone you wish of your membership.

Your name is not the only thing kept private. GA is highly private in many matters. For instance, many people believe GA is a religious organization because of its mention of a "Higher Power"—God—as a source of assistance in recovery and because many chapters meet in churches. The fact is that GA is not affiliated with any religion. Its membership is open to people of all faiths and to atheists and agnostics. The organization states in one of its informational publications that membership is open to "anyone who has a desire to stop gambling. There are no other rules and regulations concerning Gamblers Anonymous membership."

Further, GA accepts neither public funds nor contributions from outsiders to meet its financial needs. You'll also find that it does not require sign-up fees or dues of its members, and it does not demand that they support it financially in any way. The money for its operation comes from voluntary contributions by the members and chapters.

Finally GA does not take any political stand on gambling or other issues, does not participate in any public controversy, or support or oppose any cause. "Our primary purpose," says the organization, "is to stop gambling and to help other compulsives do the same."

At GA meetings the members talk of their problems and exchange information and advice with other members. At all times the aim is to help the members build a foundation for living free of gambling through what is called the Gamblers Anonymous Recovery Program. This program consists of twelve steps, or principles, and is an adaptation of the program developed and long employed by Alcoholics Anonymous. The steps are really admissions that you make to yourself and directions that you resolve to travel from now on in your life.

GA calls for you to take such actions as face your addiction and yourself squarely, admit the harm you've done, and make amends, all the while placing yourself in the hands of God, or what you understand God to be. Here, in the words of GA, are the twelve steps:

1. We admitted we were powerless over gambling—that our lives had become unmanageable.
2. Came to believe that a Power greater than ourselves could restore us to a normal way of thinking and living.
3. Made a decision to turn our will and our lives over to the care of this Power of our own understanding.
4. Made a searching and fearless moral and financial inventory of ourselves.
5. Admitted to ourselves and to another human being the exact nature of our wrongs.
6. Were entirely ready to have these defects of character removed.
7. Humbly asked God (of our understanding) to remove our shortcomings.
8. Made a list of all persons we had harmed and became willing to make amends to them all.
9. Made direct amends to such people wherever possible, except when to do so would injure them or others.
10. Continued to take personal inventory and when we were wrong, promptly admitted it.
11. Sought through prayer and meditation to improve our conscious contact with God as we understood Him, praying only for knowledge of His will for us and the power to carry that out.
12. Having made an effort to practice these principles in all our affairs, we tried to carry this message to other compulsive gamblers.

Gamblers Anonymous warns that you may fall from time to time and must be ready for those stumbles and determined to take the actions necessary to get back on your feet again. As the organization cautions its members, "To recover from one of the most baffling, insidious, compulsive addictions will require diligent effort. Honesty, open-mindedness, and willingness are the key words in our recovery."

When you are ready for GA's help, you need do no more than check your telephone directory for the number of the chapter nearest you. If no number is listed, you may call the Gamblers Anonymous International Service Office at (213) 386-8789. Should you wish to write to the Service Office, the address is P.O. Box 17173, Los Angeles, California, 90017.

♠ Gam-Anon and Gam-A-Teen

Gam-Anon and Gam-A-Teen are two organizations affiliated with Gamblers Anonymous. The former works with the compulsive's family members and friends, while the latter assists the compulsive's teenage children. Each group seeks to help its members rebuild their lives—and those of their fellow members—while the compulsive's loved ones are rebuilding theirs.

Both groups employ the twelve-step GA recovery program, but they adapt it to the special needs of their members. For example, the first step in the program for compulsives calls for them to admit that they are powerless over their gambling. For Gam-Anon and Gam-A-Teen members, however, the step is altered to read: "We admitted we were powerless over the problem in our family."

Each group encourages its members to embrace the first step as a beginning means of easing and eventually ending the feelings of guilt and helplessness felt by the families and children of compulsive gamblers. How this encouragement is offered can be seen in the guide to the twelve steps published by Gam-A-Teen for its young members. It urges them always to remember that "To admit our powerlessness over the problems we face gives us a wonderful feeling of release. We learn we are not responsible for the gambler's problem. We cannot stop the gambling, no matter how we try. We also learned we are not to blame for the gambling. With this understanding, we begin to feel free to concentrate on our own problems."

The other steps in the Gam-Anon and Gam-A-Teen programs aim to help the members better understand themselves and the compulsive in the family, to quiet the anger and frustration they have long felt, to make amends for the hurt their unhappiness has inflicted on others and on the compulsive, to restore their self-esteem, and eventually to return with the compulsive to a happy and productive life. Adults and teenagers are urged throughout their work with the two groups to live just one day at a time, slowly overcoming their problems and returning to a happy and productive life through quietly handling the challenges that each day brings.

Information on the work of Gam-Anon and Gam-A-Teen and the locations of their meeting places can be obtained by writing to the Gam-Anon International Service Office, P.O. Box 157, Whitestone, New York, 11357. The telephone number is (718) 352-1671.

While there are many hands ready to help you be free of your compulsion, there is one pair that we have yet to mention. It is perhaps the most important one of all.

It is your own.

YOUR HELPING HAND

Once you've begun to gamble, there are two things you can do to help yourself get off the road to compulsion. The first is to recognize the many danger signs that appear during the deadly three-phase pattern—among them the growing urge to gamble at all times, the urge to wager larger and larger sums, and the need to borrow or even steal the money for your next bet.

The second is to exercise the discipline and the good sense to stop immediately and break your ever-strengthening habit. Perhaps, especially if you catch yourself early enough, you'll be able to stop for good on your own. Or perhaps you'll need outside help—from your parents, your brother or sister, your closest friend, an admired teacher or religious leader, or a health professional.

But there is a problem when it comes to recognizing the danger signs. It's that old obstacle, denial. Most compulsives stubbornly and blindly deny that they are addicted—until they are near or at rock bottom. So how can you tell if you're on the road to trouble?

The fact that you're reading this book should be of help. Unlike many potential compulsives, you're learning the danger signs and so are better able to see them in yourself. Further, you're learning about the personality traits that make a person vulnerable to becoming a compulsive. Should you see these traits in yourself, you may decide to avoid experimenting with gambling in the first place.

But suppose that you fail to see or heed these warning flags. You begin to slip down through the deadly three-phase pattern, but somewhere along the line you begin to wonder if you are becoming a compulsive. How can you find out for sure? You can turn to ten questions that Gamblers Anonymous asks of teenage gamblers. Your honest answers will give you a good idea whether you're in trouble or not.

GA's Ten Questions for Teenagers

1. Have you ever stayed away from school or work to gamble?
2. Is gambling making your home life unhappy?
3. Is gambling affecting your reputation?
4. Do you ever gamble until your last dollar is gone, even your bus fare home or the cost of a burger or a Coke?
5. Have you ever lied, stolen, or borrowed just to get money to gamble?
6. Are you reluctant to spend "gambling money" on normal things?
7. After losing, do you feel you must return as soon as possible to win back your losses?
8. Is gambling more important than school or work?
9. Does gambling cause you to have difficulty in sleeping?
10. Have you ever thought of suicide as a way of solving your problems?[1]

These questions are variations, designed especially for young people, of twenty questions that Gamblers Anonymous asks of adults. Here, for your information—and to give you an idea of the extra problems you may well face should your gambling of today lead to addiction in adulthood—are those twenty questions. Most compulsive gamblers will answer yes to at least seven.

The Twenty Questions of Gamblers Anonymous

1. Did you ever lose time from work because of gambling?
2. Has gambling ever made your home life unhappy?
3. Did gambling affect your reputation?
4. Have you ever felt remorse after gambling?
5. Did you ever gamble to get money with which to pay debts or otherwise solve financial difficulties?
6. Did gambling cause a decrease in your ambition or efficiency?
7. After losing, did you feel you must return as soon as possible and win back your losses?
8. After a win did you have a strong urge to return and win more?
9. Did you often gamble until your last dollar was gone?
10. Did you ever borrow to finance your gambling?
11. Have you ever sold anything to finance your gambling?
12. Were you reluctant to use "gambling money" for normal expenditures?
13. Did gambling make you careless of the welfare of your family?
14. Did you ever gamble longer than you had planned?
15. Have you ever gambled to escape worry or trouble?
16. Have you ever committed or considered committing an illegal act to finance gambling?
17. Did gambling cause you to have difficulty sleeping?
18. Do arguments, disappointments, or frustration create within you an urge to gamble?

19. Did you ever have an urge to celebrate any good fortune by a few hours of gambling?
20. Have you ever considered self-destruction as a result of your gambling?[2]

♦ IF YOU MUST GAMBLE

As you know, millions of people gamble as a social activity without becoming compulsive. Many, however, as was said in Chapter 1, do become problem gamblers, again without developing into full-fledged compulsives. Perhaps, at times, they play more than is wise. Perhaps, on occasion, they foolishly bet more than they should and put themselves in a temporary financial bind.

You may be among those millions who are able to gamble without the threat of addiction. If so, you may still be in danger of some sort of problem gambling. You can help yourself avoid this hazard by applying and then sticking to several basic "never" and "always" rules of wise play:

> *Never* risk all of your money when gambling or when making a single bet. Always leave some at home or in the bank. If you're in a faraway place, be sure to set some aside for your trip home. Then never pull it out of your pocket.

> *Never* gamble more than you can afford.

> *Always* set a limit on the amount of money you can afford to lose. When you've lost that amount, don't go looking for more. Forget about doing more gambling. Go home or to the movies.

> *Always* set a limit on the amount of time you plan to spend on a gambling session. Very often, the longer you play, the more likely you are to lose.

> *Never* borrow money to gamble.

Never think that, because you win right away, you're going to win all the time.

Never send good money after bad. When you're losing, don't increase your wagers in the hope of winning everything back at once. It almost never works.

Always learn something about the gambling game in which you're going to participate. This is essential if the game requires skill on your part. Ignorance of a game means poor play. Poor play almost invariably means that you'll lose.

There are, as reported in Chapter 1, an estimated 8 to 10 million compulsive gamblers in the United States today. Predictions are that gambling, which is now being legalized in more and more locales, is sure to spread to every corner of the country in the years to come. This means that increasing numbers of Americans, many of whom once shunned gambling because it was illegal or because it violated their moral principles, will try their hand at the various kinds of play that are legally available. In turn, this means that the number of compulsives—young people among them—is certain to grow as the years pass.

The nation at present is said to be in the grip of a gambling fever. Experts in gambling problems are predicting that compulsive gambling will become a major youth problem—even *the* major youth problem—of the 1990s. They call it a growing American tragedy.

If you are at all vulnerable to compulsive gambling, you are in danger of becoming a part of this tragedy. If so, no matter what suggestions may be given for wise gambling, there is only one rule that will work for you: **Don't even think about starting**.

SOURCE NOTES

♠ **Chapter One:**
Teenage Gambling

1. Jan's story is by a member of Gamblers Anonymous; Ben's story is from R. Chavira, "The Rise of Teenage Gambling," *Time*, February 25, 1991, p. 78.
2. A. Levine, "Playing the Adolescent Odds," *U.S. News & World Report*, June 18, 1990, p. 51.
3. The material on the current spread of legal gambling in the United States is developed from G. J. Church, "Why Pick on Pete?" *Time*, July 10, 1989, pp. 17–18; S. Donoghue and S. Monroe, "The States Like the Odds," *Time*, July 10, 1989; P. Glastris and A. Bates, "The Fool's Gold in Gambling," *U.S. News & World Report*, April 1, 1991; V. C. Lorenz, "Family Dynamics of Pathological Gamblers," in *The Handbook of Pathological Gambling* (Springfield, Ill.: Charles C. Thomas, 1987), p. 72; P. G. Satre, "The Future of Gambling: You Can Bet on It," *Vital Speeches*

of the Day, April 1, 1990, pp. 364–65; G. F. Will, "In the Grip of Gambling," *Newsweek*, May 8, 1989, p. 78.

4. The material on the studies made of youth gambling is developed from G. Boeck, "High School Students Are Unnoticed Victims of Pervasive Gambling," *USA Today*, March 26, 1991; M. D. riffiths, "Gambling in Children and Adolescents," *Journal of Gambling Behavior*, Spring 1988, pp. 68–70; S. G. Ide-Smith and S.E.G. Lea, "Gambling in Young Adolescents," *Journal of Gambling Behavior*, Summer 1988, pp. 110, 114; R. Ladouceur and C. Mireault, "Gambling Behaviors among High School Students in the Quebec Area," *Journal of Gambling Behavior*, Spring 1988, p. 6; H. R. Lesieur and R. Klein, "Pathological Gambling among High School Students," *Addictive Behaviors*, Volume 12, 1987, p. 130; Levine, p. 51; M. Winter, "Lotto Fever Enjoyable for Some but for Others It's Real Sickness," *Fresno* (California) *Bee*, April 17, 1991; C. Yingst, "Lottery Fever Promotes Teenage Addiction, Psychologist Reports," *The Sun* (southern California), April 18, 1991.

5. The material on the number of underage gamblers refused entry to or ejected from New Jersey casinos is developed from Chavira, p. 78; G. McCabe, "Too Young to Gamble," *Las Vegas Review-Journal*, June 14, 1990; *Youth and Gambling*, a fact sheet published by the National Council on Problem Gambling, undated.

6. The material on the number of compulsive gamblers in the United States is developed from Chavira, p. 78; R. Custer and H. Milt, *When Luck Runs Out: Help for Compulsive Gamblers and Their Families* (New York: Facts on File, 1985), p. 40; V. C. Lorenz, *An Overview of Pathological*

Gambling, a report issued by the National Center for Pathological Gambling, January 1990, p. 3.
7. Chavira, p. 78.
8. Ibid.
9. Ibid.
10. Ibid.
11. The material on the Atlantic City teenage girl is developed from Chavira, p. 78; Levine, p. 51.

♥ Chapter Two:
Gambling through the Ages
1. The material in the section "Gambling after the Written Word" is developed from P. Arnold, *The Encyclopedia of Gambling* (Secaucus, N.J.: Chartwell Books, 1977), pp. 13, 21, 25; R. Cavendish, editor, *Man, Myth & Magic: An Illustrated Encyclopedia of the Supernatural* (New York: Marshall Cavendish, 1970), Volume 8, pp. 1060–61; *New Larousse Encyclopedia of Mythology*, 1989 edition (New York: Crescent Books, 1989), pp. 15–16; M. Leach, editor, *Funk & Wagnall's Standard Dictionary of Folklore, Mythology and Legend* (New York: Harper & Row, 1972), p. 431; H. S. Robinson and K. Wilson, *Myths and Legends of All Nations* (Garden City, N.J.: Garden City Books, 1960), pp. 2, 3, 6; J. Scarne, *Scarne's Complete Guide to Gambling* (New York: Simon & Schuster, 1961), pp. 125–26, 527–28; A. Wykes, *The Complete Illustrated Guide to Gambling* (New York: Doubleday, 1964), pp. 28–31, 35, 37, 38–41, 134.
2. The material in the section "Centuries of Gambling" is developed from Scarne, pp. 12–13, 39, 59, 528; Wykes, p. 33.
3. The material in the section "Centuries of Criticism" is developed from R. Sasuly, *Bookies &*

Bettors: Two Hundred Years of Gambling (New York: Holt, Rinehart & Winston, 1982), pp. 40–41; Wykes, pp. 35–36.

♠ **Chapter Three:**
Gambling in the United States

1. A. Fleming, *Something for Nothing: A History of Gambling* (New York: Delacorte, 1978), p. 18; J. Scarne, *Scarne's Complete Guide to Gambling* (New York: Simon & Schuster, 1961), p. 533.

2. The material in the section "Gambling in Colonial America" is developed from P. Arnold, *The Encyclopedia of Gambling* (Secaucus, N.J.: Chartwell Books, 1977) pp. 173–74; Fleming, p. 7; P. G. Satre, "The Future of Gambling: You Can Bet on It," *Vital Speeches of the Day*, April 1, 1990, p. 365; Scarne, pp. 129, 135–36, 533–36.

3. The material in the section "Gambling in the Young United States" is developed from Arnold, pp. 209–18; Editors of Time-Life Books, *The Gamblers* (Alexandria, Va.: Time-Life Books, 1978), pp. 159–61, 169, 176, 221–22; S. Longstreet, *Win or Lose: A Social History of Gambling in America* (Indianapolis: Bobbs-Merrill, 1976), pp. 31, 36; R. Sasuly, *Bookies and Bettors: Two Hundred Years of Gambling* (New York: Holt, Rinehart & Winston, 1982), p. 68; A. Wykes, *The Complete Illustrated Guide to Gambling* (New York: Doubleday, 1964), pp. 25–26, 44, 263–64, 308–9.

4. The material in the section "A Gambling Fever" is developed from Arnold, p. 26; Satre, pp. 365, 366; Wykes, pp. 299–300, 302.

5. The material in the section "Gambling in America Today" is developed from three fact sheets published by the National Council on Problem Gambling: *Some Casino Facts, Some Lottery*

Facts, and *Some Parimutuel Facts,* all undated; Satre, pp. 365–66.

♦ **Chapter Four:**
The Compulsive Gambler

1. M. D. Griffiths, "Gambling in Children and Adolescents," *Journal of Gambling Behavior,* Spring 1989, p. 71.
2. The material in the section "Who Are the Compulsive Gamblers?" is developed from *Your Lucky Number,* a television documentary produced by MPT Productions, Owings Mills, Maryland, 1988, transcript, p. 9; *Final Report: Task Force on Gambling Addiction in Maryland,* Maryland Department of Health and Mental Hygiene, Alcohol and Drug Abuse Administration, 1990, p. 20; V. C. Lorenz, *The Compulsive Gambling Hotline: FY90 Final Report,* National Center for Pathological Gambling, August 1990, p. 6; Lorenz, "State Lotteries and Compulsive Gambling," *Journal of Gambling Studies,* Winter 1990, p. 385; *Overview of Compulsive Gambling,* a fact sheet published by the National Council on Problem Gambling, undated.
3. The material in the section "Compulsive Gambling: An Illness" is developed from R. Custer and H. Milt, *When Luck Runs Out: Help for Compulsive Gamblers and Their Families* (New York: Facts on File, 1985), pp. 35–37; H. R. Lesieur, *Understanding Compulsive Gambling* (Center City, Minn.: Hazelden Foundation, 1986), p. 3.
4. The material in the section "You As a Compulsive Gambler" is developed from *Final Report: Task Force,* pp. 22–23; Custer and Milt, pp. 57–61, 63–67; H. R. Lesieur, *The Female Pathological Gambler,* a paper presented at the seventh

International Conference on Gambling and Risk Taking, Reno, Nevada, August 1987; Lesieur, *Understanding Compulsive Gambling*, pp. 2–3; R. A. McCormick and J. I. Taber, "The Pathological Gambler: Salient Personality Traits," in *The Handbook of Pathological Gambling* (Springfield, Ill.: Charles C. Thomas, 1987), p. 16.

♣ **Chapter Five:**
The Deadly Pattern

1. The material in the section "Phase 1: The Beginning" is developed from R. Custer and H. Milt, *When Luck Runs Out: Help for Compulsive Gamblers and Their Families* (New York: Facts on File, 1985), pp. 99–105; *Final Report: Task Force on Gambling Addiction in Maryland*, Department of Mental Health and Hygiene, Drug Abuse Administration, 1990, p. 25; H. R. Lesieur, *Understanding Compulsive Gambling* (Center City, Minn.: Hazelden Foundation, 1986); Lesieur, *The Female Pathological Gambler*, a paper presented at the seventh International Conference on Gambling and Risk Taking, Reno, Nevada, August 1987.

2. The material in the section "Phase 2: Now You're Losing" is developed from Custer and Milt, pp. 105–12; *Final Report: Task Force*, pp. 25–26; Lesieur, *Understanding Compulsive Gambling*, pp. 5–6.

3. The material in the section "Phase 3: Gambling Desperately" is developed from Custer and Milt, pp. 112–21; *Final Report: Task Force*, pp. 26–27; H. R. Lesieur, *The Chase: Career of the Compulsive Gambler* (Rochester, Vt.: Schenkman Books, 1984), pp. 227–28; *Your Lucky Number*, a television documentary produced by MPT Pro-

ductions, Owings Mills, Maryland, 1988, transcript, pp. 17–18.

♥ **Chapter Six:**
Hitting Rock Bottom

1. R. Custer, "The Diagnosis and Scope of Pathological Gambling," in *The Handbook of Pathological Gambling* (Springfield, Ill.: Charles C. Thomas, 1987), p. 6.
2. The material in the section "Your Health" is developed from H. R. Lesieur, *The Female Pathological Gambler*, a paper presented at the seventh International Conference on Gambling and Risk Taking, Reno, Nevada, August 1987; V. C. Lorenz and R. A. Yaffee, "Pathological Gambling: Psychosomatic, Emotional and Marital Difficulties as Reported by the Gambler," *Journal of Gambling Behavior*, Spring-Summer 1986, pp. 41–44; *Psychiatric Illnesses Suffered by Compulsive Gamblers*, a fact sheet published by the National Council on Problem Gambling, undated.
3. The material in the section "Dual Addiction" is developed from J. Ciarrocchi, "Severity of Impairment in Dually Addicted Gamblers," *Journal of Gambling Behavior*, Spring 1987, pp. 16, 19, 22; Lesieur, *The Female Pathological Gambler; Dual Addiction among Compulsive Gamblers*, a fact sheet published by the National Council on Problem Gambling, undated.
4. The material in the section "Suicide" is developed from R. Custer and H. Milt, *When Luck Runs Out: Help for Compulsive Gamblers and Their Families* (New York: Facts on File, 1985), p. 121; H. R. Lesieur, *The Chase: Career of the Compulsive Gambler* (Rochester, Vt.: Schenkman Books, 1984), pp. 235–36; Lesieur, *Understanding*

Compulsive Gambling (Center City, Minn.: Hazelden Foundation, 1986), p. 7; *Suicide among Pathological Gamblers*, a fact sheet published by the National Council on Problem Gambling, undated.

♠ **Chapter Seven:**
Your Family: At Rock Bottom with You
1. The material in the section "Your Parents" is developed from V. C. Lorenz, "Family Dynamics of Pathological Gamblers," in *The Handbook of Pathological Gambling* (Springfield, Ill.: Charles C. Thomas, 1987), pp. 79–82.
2. The material in the section "Your Spouse" is developed from R. Custer and H. Milt, *When Luck Runs Out: Help for Compulsive Gamblers and Their Families* (New York: Facts on File, 1985), pp. 123–24, 125–29, 134–37, 140–42, 144–45, 147; H. R. Lesieur, *Understanding Compulsive Gambling* (Center City, Minn.: Hazelden Foundation, 1986), p. 11; Lorenz and R. A. Yaffee, "Pathological Gambling: Psychosomatic, Emotional and Marital Difficulties as Reported by the Spouse," *Journal of Gambling Behavior*, Spring 1988, pp. 13–20; Lorenz, "Family Dynamics," pp. 74–75, 76–79; *Social Costs of Compulsive Gambling*, a fact sheet published by the National Council on Problem Gambling, undated.
3. The material in the section "Your Children" is developed from Custer and Milt, pp. 137–39; D. F. Jacobs, A. R. Marston, R. D. Singer, K. Widaman, T. Little, and J. Veizades, "Children of Pathological Gamblers," *Journal of Gambling Behavior*, Winter 1989, pp. 261–64, 265–66; Lorenz, "Family Dynamics," pp. 83–84; H. R. Lesieur and J. Rothschild, "Children of Gamblers Anonymous Members," *Journal of Gam-*

bling Behavior, Winter 1989, pp. 269–73; *Youth and Gambling,* a fact sheet published by the National Council on Problem Gambling, undated.

◆ **Chapter Eight:**
The Road Back
1. The material in the section "The Three-Phase Pattern of Recovery" is developed from R. Custer, "The Diagnosis and Scope of Pathological Gambling," in *The Handbook of Pathological Gambling* (Springfield, Ill.: Charles C. Thomas, 1987), p. 7.
2. *Gamblers Anonymous,* an informational publication of Gamblers Anonymous, undated, p. 13.
3. *Therapists Referral,* an informational publication of the National Council on Problem Gambling, undated.
4. The material in the section "Hospital and Health Center Treatment Programs is developed from J. I. Tabor and R. A. McCormick, "The Pathological Gambler in Treatment," in *The Handbook of Pathological Gambling,* pp. 144, 155; *Compulsive Gambling Rehabilitation Program,* an informational publication by Charter Hospital, Las Vegas, undated, p. 3; *List of Treatment Programs for Compulsive Gambling,* an informational publication of the National Council on Problem Gambling, undated.
5. The material in the section "Gamblers Anonymous" is developed from two publications by Gamblers Anonymous, *Gamblers Anonymous: Questions and Answers about the Problem of Compulsive Gambling and the G.A. Recovery Program,* undated, pp. 1–7, and *GA: Gamblers Anonymous,* undated, p. 1, and from three informational booklets published by the Gam-Anon International Service Office: *Gam-Anon: 12 Steps*

to Recovery, 1989, p. 1; *Gam-Anon Family Groups: The Gam-Anon Way of Life*, 1988, pp. 3, 4; and *Gam-A-Teen*, p. 3. In addition, certain material in the section was supplied to the author in telephone conversations with Karen H., international executive secretary, Gamblers Anonymous.

♣ **Chapter Nine:**
Your Helping Hand
1. *Gamblers Anonymous: Young Gamblers in Recovery*, a publication of Gamblers Anonymous, undated, pp. 1–2.
2. *The Twenty Questions of Gamblers Anonymous, A Fact Sheet Published by Gamblers Anonymous*, undated.

BIBLIOGRAPHY

♥ **Books**

Arnold, Peter. *The Encyclopedia of Gambling.* Secaucus, New Jersey: Chartwell Books, 1977.

Bergler, Edmund. *The Psychology of Gambling.* New York: International Universities Press, 1970.

Cavendish, Richard, Editor. *Man, Myth & Magic: An Illustrated Encyclopedia of the Supernatural,* Volume 8. New York: Marshall Cavendish, 1970.

Custer, Robert, and Milt, Harry. *When Luck Runs Out: Help for Compulsive Gamblers and Their Families.* New York: Facts on File, 1985.

Editors of Time-Life Books. *The Gamblers.* Alexandria, Virginia: Time-Life Books, 1978.

Fleming, Alice. *Something for Nothing: A History of Gambling.* New York: Delacorte, 1978.

Galski, Thomas, Editor. *The Handbook of Pathological Gambling.* Springfield, Illinois: Charles C. Thomas, 1987.

Leach, Maria, Editor. *Funk & Wagnall's Standard*

Dictionary of Folklore, Mythology and Legend.
New York: Harper & Row, 1972.

Lesieur, Henry R. *The Chase: Career of the Compulsive Gambler.* Rochester, Vermont: Schenkman Books, 1984.

Longstreet, Stephen. *Win or Lose: A Social History of Gambling in America.* Indianapolis: Bobbs-Merrill, 1977.

New Larousse Encyclopedia of Mythology. New York: Crescent Books, 1989.

Robinson, Herbert Spencer, and Wilson, Knox. *Myths and Legends of All Nations.* Garden City, New York: Garden City Books, 1960.

Sasuly, Richard. *Bookies & Bettors: Two Hundred Years of Gambling.* New York: Holt, Rinehart & Winston, 1982.

Scarne, John. *Scarne's Complete Guide to Gambling.* New York: Simon & Schuster, 1961.

Wykes, Alan. *The Complete Illustrated Guide to Gambling.* New York: Doubleday, 1964.

♠ **Booklets**

Gam-Anon: 12 Steps to Recovery. Whitestone, New York: Gam-Anon International Services Office, 1989.

Games Compulsive Gamblers and We Play. Whitestone, New York: Gam-Anon International Service Office, 1971.

Lesieur, Henry R. *Understanding Compulsive Gambling.* Center City, Minnesota: Hazelden Foundation, 1986.

Lorenz, Valerie C. *Releasing Guilt.* Center City, Minnesota: Hazelden Foundation, 1988.

———*Standing Up to Fear.* Center City, Minnesota: Hazelden Foundation, 1989.

◆ **Professional Journals**

Ciarrocchi, Joseph. "Severity of Impairment in Dually Addicted Gamblers," *Journal of Gambling Behavior*, Spring 1987.

Frank, Michael L., and Smith, Crystal. "Illusion of Control and Gambling in Children," *Journal of Gambling Behavior*, Summer 1989.

Griffiths, Mark D. "Gambling in Children and Adolescents," *Journal of Gambling Behavior*, Spring 1989.

Ide-Smith, Susan G., and Lea, Stephen E. G. "Gambling in Young Adolescents," *Journal of Gambling Behavior*, Summer 1988.

Jacobs, Durand F., Marston, Albert R., Singer, Robert D., Widaman, Keith, and Veizades, Jeannette, "Children of Problem Gamblers," *Journal of Gambling Behavior*, Winter 1989.

Ladouceur, Robert, and Mireault, Chantal. "Gambling Behavior among High School Students in the Quebec Area," *Journal of Gambling Behavior*, Spring 1988.

Lesieur, Henry R., and Rothschild, Jerome. "Children of Gamblers Anonymous Members," *Journal of Gambling Behavior*, Winter 1989.

Lesieur, Henry R., and Klein, Robert. "Pathological Gambling Among High School Students," *Addictive Behaviors*, Volume 12, 1987.

Lorenz, Valerie C., and Yaffe, Robert A. "Pathological Gambling: Psychosomatic, Emotional and Marital Difficulties as Reported by the Gambler," *Journal of Gambling Behavior*, Spring-Summer 1986.

————. "Pathological Gambling: Psychosomatic, Emotional and Marital Difficulties as Reported by the Spouse." *Journal of Gambling Behavior*, Spring 1988.

————. "Pathological Gamblers and Their Spouses: Problems in Interaction." *Journal of Gambling Behavior,* Summer 1989.

♣ General Periodicals

Berkman, Sue. "When Gambling Becomes a Disease," *Good Housekeeping,* January, 1991.

Bruner, Kathleen. "High Stakes: The Number of Teen Gamblers in the United States Is Rising at an Alarming Rate," *Gambling,* May 1989.

Chivara, Ricardo. "The Rise of Teenage Gambling," *Time,* February 25, 1991.

Church, George. "Why Pick on Pete?" *Time,* July 10, 1989.

Donoghue, Shelagh. "The States Like the Odds," *Time,* July 10, 1989.

Glastris, Paul, and Bates, Andrew. "The Fool's Gold in Gambling: States Learn How Hard It Is to Control Gaming," *U.S. News & World Report,* April 1, 1991.

Levine, Art. "Playing the Adolescent Odds," *U.S. News & World Report,* June 18, 1990.

Satre, Philip G. "The Future of Gambling: You Can Bet on It," *Vital Speeches of the Day,* April 1, 1990.

Shaw, Bill. "Vegas, Atlantic City and Now . . . Deadwood, South Dakota, Where Gambling Is a Very Big Deal," *People,* April 1, 1991.

Will, George. "In the Grip of Gambling," *Newsweek,* May 8, 1989.

♥ Studies, Papers, and Reports

Final Report: Task Force on Gambling Addiction in Maryland. Baltimore: Maryland Department of Health and Mental Hygiene, Alcohol and Drug Abuse Administration, 1990.

Lesieur, Henry R. *The Female Pathological Gam-*

bler, a paper presented at the seventh International Conference on Gambling and Risk Taking, Reno, Nevada, August 1987.

Lorenz, Valerie C. *The Compulsive Gambling Hotline: FY90 Final Report.* Baltimore: The National Center for Pathological Gambling, August 1990.

♠ **Newspapers**

Jacobs, Durand. "High School Students Are Unnoticed Victims of Pervasive Problem," *USA Today,* March 26, 1991.

Libman, Gary. "Compulsive Gambling: A New Round of Victims," *Los Angeles Times,* March 28, 1989.

McCabe, George. "Too Young to Gamble," *Las Vegas Review-Journal,* June 14, 1990.

Winter, Michael. "Lotto Fever Enjoyable for Some but for Others It's Real Sickness," *Fresno* (California) *Bee,* April 17, 1991.

Yingst, Cindy. "Lottery Fever Promotes Teenage Addiction, Psychologist Reports," *The Sun* (southern California), April 18, 1991.

♦ **Television Transcript**

Your Lucky Number, MPT Productions, Owings Mills, Maryland.

♣ **Special Publications**

Fact sheets published by the National Council on Problem Gambling:
   Some Casino Facts
   Some Lottery Facts
   Some Parimutuel Facts
   Overview of Compulsive Gambling
   Social Costs of Compulsive Gambling
   Characteristics and Behaviors of Compulsive Gamblers

Women and Gambling
Youth and Gambling
Physical Illnesses Suffered by Compulsive Gamblers and Spouses of Gamblers
Psychiatric Illnesses Suffered by Compulsive Gamblers
Suicide among Compulsive Gamblers
Dual Addiction among Compulsive Gamblers
Crime and Compulsive Gambling
Spouses of Compulsive Gamblers
Compulsive Gambling and Family Violence
Informational material published by Gamblers Anonymous:
Gamblers Anonymous: Questions and Answers about the Problem of Compulsive Gambling and the G.A. Recovery Program
Gamblers Anonymous: Young Gamblers in Recovery
Informational material published by Gam-Anon:
Gam-Anon: 12 Steps to Recovery
Gam-Anon Family Groups: The Gam-Anon Way of Life
Gam-A-Teen

INDEX

ABOUT THE AUTHOR

Edward F. Dolan is the award-winning author of nearly ninety nonfiction books for young people and adults. His recent books for Franklin Watts include *The American Wilderness and Its Future: Conservation Versus Use, Drugs in Sports: Revised Edition, America After Vietnam: Legacies of a Hated War,* and *Child Abuse, Revised Edition.*

Mr. Dolan lives in Novato, California.